A STRANGER'S PROMISE

LORDS OF CHANCE BOOK ONE

TARAH SCOTT

CLAIRMONT HOUSE

CHAPTER 1

London, February 1814

"Scandalous." Captain Edwards sniffed in disdain. Charlotte tried not to wince when he turned his icy gaze from the store window to her. "No wife of mine would even *look* at such a gown." His bearded jaw clenched, he added in an even stronger censorious tone, "Frankly, Charlotte, I am disappointed."

We aren't married—yet, Charlotte retorted in her mind, and caught herself mid-roll of her eyes.

She pushed her prim straw bonnet back from her face and turned back to the shop window for another look. The gown floated there like a dream come true. Cut in the latest fashion and trimmed with embroidered rosebuds, lace, and tiny seed pearls, its sweeping, crimson silk skirt fell in a tumble of soft, sensuous folds. The dressmaker had even angled several mirrors around the masterpiece to highlight the different views.

Charlotte grinned. If she squinted her eyes and tilted her

head just a little to the left, she could almost imagine herself wearing the confection. In her mind's eye, an obliging shaft of winter sunlight caught the playful spark in her eyes along with the brilliant gold of her unruly brown curls, a contrast against the cream taffeta as she whirled in the dress.

Her future husband's heavy hand fell upon her shoulder. She jarred back into the moment and caught his reflection in the window. A toned and muscular tower of a man, resplendent in a Queen's fine scarlet coat with its gold braid and polished brass buttons. A gallantly handsome figure, to be sure —at first glance, anyway. A deeper inspection revealed chilling blue eyes and the vein on his forehead pulsed in disapproval, a vein that betrayed an ever-present simmering rage.

"I insist we leave, Charlotte." He grasped her arm. "A virtuous woman would never soil her father's good name—nor *mine*—by wearing such an abomination."

Charlotte suppressed a snort. "I merely thought it pretty, Captain Edwards."

"As my future wife, I insist you think no such thing." He looped his arm through hers and pulled her away from the shop window.

This time, she did roll her eyes. Heavens, did the man seek to control her thoughts? She snorted.

Captain Edwards paused midstride and peered down at her through narrowed eyes. "Are you mocking me?"

Charlotte thinned her lips in a grim line. She'd witnessed the Captain's temper often enough to regret her acceptance of his marriage proposal—a proposal her father had pressured her to accept at the tender age of sixteen. Her father, a major in the Queen's army, found Captain Edwards quite the catch. Not only was he a decorated captain, but a distant cousin to a baronet. Later, she learned her father owed the man a great deal of money. The discovery gave her courage. She'd begged her father to allow her to end the engagement, but he thought it far too late, and reminded her that he valued loyalty and faithfulness above all else—after the balance of his bank account, of course.

Still, she tried to change his mind, but whenever she broached the matter, he invariably replied, "It is *you* who must change, Charlotte. You are proud and willful. Be grateful the man still wants you. Heed his guidance. Marriage isn't pleasure. Marriage is work. When you're older, you'll understand. Now, *enough* of this foolishness."

Well, now she was older and she understood very well. Her father sought only to protect his own interests—not hers.

"*I am speaking to you, Charlotte.*" Captain Edwards gave her arm a rough shake. "I repeat, are you mocking me?"

Charlotte blinked. She cleared her throat, then answered in the most placating of tones, "No, sir."

He searched her face, clearly—and rightly—suspicious of her sincerity before nodding in satisfaction. Anchoring her arm tightly under his, he resumed their walk down the icy, snow-covered street.

"I know you think me harsh, Charlotte," he said. "But I've only your best interests at heart. Be grateful I am here to guide you. Because of me, you have blossomed into a virtuous woman, a woman worthy of becoming my wife. You've changed so much from when I met you as an undisciplined young girl of fifteen."

Charlotte looked away, in an effort to keep her anger in check. If only she *hadn't* met him that summer six years ago, that dreadful day when he'd first stepped foot in her father's home. She'd been far too young and impressionable to see what he truly was: an insufferable, judgmental boor of a prig— and a prig with a raging temper at that.

"Now, you are of an age where one expects you to have overcome your flaws," he droned on, puffing his chest pompously with each judging word. "The unhappy catastrophe of your mother's death as a child resulted in your lack of a proper upbringing, but…"

Charlotte let his voice fade into the background and took a deep lungful of the crisp, clean winter air. She'd heard this speech countless times. Her mother had died in childbirth, leaving her newborn daughter with only a name and a leather-bound cookery book. And with her father stationed in far-off India, Charlotte and cookbook passed between various family members for a time. She'd finally found a happy home with an elderly, distant relative, a retired Navy man who taught her Greek philosophy and the fine art of swearing. She'd been delightfully happy. Then he passed away and shortly after, her father returned from abroad.

"A humble, subservient wife, Charlotte," the pompous man at her side continued. "One who wears only *modest* attire. You must be the very model of propriety…"

A dark cloud passed over the sun. Stifling a yawn, Charlotte stared at the sudden snowflakes swirling down from above and tracked their descent from the sky as they flurried around the streetlamps along the lane. If only she could be as free to simply float away.

"Respect, duty, and honor," Captain Edwards kept on. "Discipline and fortitude. A woman to remain by my side through life's fortunes and misfortunes. Do you not agree that these are the obligations of a proper wife, Charlotte?"

"Yes, sir," she mumbled dutifully.

A break in the buildings ahead offered a sudden tantalizing glimpse of the Frost Fair spread out on the frozen Thames below. She'd read about it in the papers, but in person, it was fabulous, a living painting of women in brightly beribboned, feathered bonnets, men in velvet top hats, and children skating on the ice, toffee apples in hand. Painters lined the river banks, squinted in the darkening afternoon with brushes in hand as they captured the gaiety of the wondrous occasion on their canvases. Men on stilts threaded through the crowds gathered to watch the puppet shows and gape at the elephant by Black Friar's Bridge, used periodically to test the strength of the ice.

Suddenly, Captain Edwards cupped her chin and forced her eyes up to his. "What do you say to that?" he asked in a deep voice.

Charlotte blinked, startled by the unexpectedness of his move. He usually railed on for a good half hour or so. She twisted her lips and tried in vain to recall his words. "*Da*—uh… dare I agree, sir?" She caught herself at the last second and swiftly changed *damnation* into *dare*.

His blue eyes remained aloof, cool, and critical. She bit her lip, in hopes her reply a sufficient one to whatever he'd asked.

His lips spread into a slow smile. "I am pleased, Charlotte."

She let out a breath of relief.

"Then we agree," he said. "We will wed this summer. At last."

Charlotte choked. *This summer?*

"Charlotte!" a woman's frantic voice called from behind. "*Charlotte!*"

Charlotte whirled. The butcher's wife waved her apron as she ran toward them, sliding in the icy snow.

"Go home, girl, home. At once," the woman wheezed as she arrived. "It's Major Atchenson, your father. There's been an accident."

An accident. Two simple words that changed Charlotte's life forever.

Alone in the empty London townhouse, Charlotte huddled next to the kitchen stove in a solemn mood, as howling winds brought more snow. The coal hadn't lasted more than a week after her father's death. Unable to afford more, she'd resorted to what wood she could find, but with harsh winter weather, everyone in London searched as well, and she found precious little. She'd been reduced to buying twisted sticks of soiled straw from the hotel stables at the end of the lane, but it flamed so fast it provided little heat.

Now, she stared at the stove, wondering what she had left to burn. The creditors had taken everything.

Well…she had her relatives' letters.

With a bitter, mirthless smile, she tossed them into the stove, lit the match, then watched the heartless missives catch fire, all of them variations of the same *we cannot provide any assistance...* Cannot or will not? It didn't matter. She'd find her own way.

Shawl drawn tight around her shoulders, Charlotte remained seated before the stove long after the last letter curled into ash. She now understood the meaning of 'nightmare.' She'd been living in one the past few weeks.

"An accident," the constable had called her father's death. He'd fallen through the ice and drowned in the Thames. She hadn't believed them. She still didn't. Not after seeing the elephant standing on the river ice that very same day. How could her father break ice that could withstand the weight of an elephant? The idea stretched the imagination beyond credibility, but what could she do? No one cared—even *before* the creditors descended upon her like wild dogs.

Tears wet her lashes. She'd returned from the churchyard, having just seen her father buried, to find the creditors hovering like vultures at the townhouse's front door.

"What is this?" Captain Edwards had stepped to the forefront of the funeral party to confront the men. "What business have you here?"

They'd answered that their business concerned promissory notes long past due and letters from banks with demands for immediate compensation to the sum of several thousand pounds. At that, every head in the funeral party had turned.

Tongues tutted. Captain Edwards' mouth had dropped open in shock.

"Gaming debts," someone said.

"A swindler," said another.

"Scandal," they all agreed.

The creditors took everything. Even her mother's leather-bound cookery book.

Charlotte couldn't recall much after that, except for the beauty of the snowflakes swirling down from the sky to gently kiss her tear-stained cheeks.

The ring of St. Clement's bells in the distance jolted her back to the present.

"You weep more for the cookery book than your fiancé, Charlotte." She laughed bitterly and drew in a long, shaky breath.

Just an hour ago, Captain Edwards stood in the kitchen and commented on the lack of coal. He then handed her the last letter, saying, "As you know, Miss Atchenson, a man of my position must choose his wife with care, a woman from an upstanding family. I have done all I can for you."

Charlotte had stared in surprise. Yes, he'd stood by her side as they'd lowered her father into his grave, but so had many others. He'd done precious little else—ah, besides deliver the letter.

"I shall not marry you. I cannot besmirch my good name," he'd continued, pompous to the end. "Your father...well, the evidence of his scandalous behavior is undeniable." She stood frozen as he pulled a small leather bag from his waistcoat and tossed it at her feet. "This is my final act of kindness. Ten shillings."

Ten? Ten shillings? Fury swept through her anew at the memory of how she'd grabbed the bag from the floor, slapped it hard against his chest, and shouted, "What use have I for ten shillings when I have more than a thousand demands for the paltry sum?" She hadn't stopped there. She'd said the words she'd longed to say for years, "You are an arrogant ass, a fool and a bully. How thankful I am to not wed such a cruel, heartless and hypocritical man. Not even a month ago, did you not speak to me of respect, duty, and honor? Discipline? Of standing by your side through all the trials of life's fortunes and misfortunes? Or is it only the woman who must remain faithful?"

A dark color had stained his cheeks and he'd raised his hand. She took a faltering step back, then caught herself.

They stared at one another for several long moments before his hand slowly dropped. "Do not seek me out, Charlotte. I shall no longer acknowledge you." Then he left, his pittance clutched in his hand.

Charlotte smiled at the ashes inside the stove. Despite her destitute circumstances, she couldn't deny the sense of freedom, the weight that had been lifted from her shoulders. "You should've taken the coins, Charlotte," she criticized with a rueful shake of her head. "Ten shillings are better than none when you've eaten the last of the salted haddock and every doorstep you've stood on has turned you away."

She'd been unable to find work, even as a scullery maid.

With a sigh, she rose and stalked to the empty parlor with its undressed windows, for the creditors had taken even the worn damask curtains. She leaned her forehead against the frozen windowpane and looked out at the winter stillness blanketing the city. Only the streetlamps shone like beacons in the night.

"Tomorrow." She clenched her hands in determination. "Tomorrow this nightmare will end."

Tomorrow she would find employment. She had to. If she didn't, she'd be forced out onto London's frozen streets or into debtor's prison in less than a week, since her father still owed more than what his life had been worth.

CHAPTER 2

ALISTAIR JAMES, BARON AISLA, 11TH EARL OF CASSILIS, AND Laird of Castle Culzean, made quite the formidable picture standing before the fireplace in his aunt's Mayfair townhouse parlor. Dressed in a stylish, dark blue waistcoat with a silk cravat tied in the latest fashion, the handsome Scottish lord loomed tall, broad-shouldered, and muscular in an elegantly lean way. His bright green eyes and dimpled chin, combined with the sensual curl of his lip, made him the talk of the town—particularly since he rarely graced it with his presence. His aunt had spent the last ten minutes harping on this very subject instead of discussing the real matter at hand.

"And shall we now discuss the governesses you have chosen?" he at last interjected. "On my honor, I will no' have a one of them." Alistair pressed his mouth into a firm line of disapproval. He raised an elegant hand to cut his aunt's diatribe short. "Hags. The lot of them."

Lady Prescott's eyes popped in surprise. "Hags?" she gasped. "The last *two* governesses brought impeccable letters of recommendation, Alistair. Lady *Boswell's* recommendations, no less."

Alistair let the mocking arch of his brow express his

opinion of Lady Boswell, by far the cruelest gossipmonger in the *ton*—after his aunt, of course. He eyed the woman as she sat on her gilded, brocade chair like a queen on her throne, her aged face a mask of dissatisfaction and her mouth set in a permanent, judgmental frown. He held nothing in common with her—or any of his father's kin, for that matter.

"Frankly, why do you bother?" His aunt waved her Spanish, black-lace fan. "The children are…" Her voice trailed away and her nostrils flared again, this time in distaste.

Alistair pinned her with a stare. "The children are?" he prompted.

Lady Prescott knew better than to answer. "I would think *you* would understand," she huffed instead and, unable to bear his stern gaze, glanced away.

"Oh, I understand," he replied in a lethally soft voice. "I truly do."

The old woman stiffened. "Your situation was entirely different from theirs. Your mother was…was…well, your father wed her, did he not? In the end? Even though she was nothing but a scullery maid."

Nothing but a scullery maid. How many times had he felt the stinging slap of those words? Yes, in the end, his father *had* set things right, but the final act of legitimizing his estranged, eldest son hadn't stemmed from honor or remorse. His father simply had no choice—not if he wished his legacy to survive. Obsessed with rebuilding Castle Culzean at the expense of all else, the old earl had bankrupted his entire estate. It was either recognize Alistair—and the vast fortune he'd accumulated in his own right, a fortune that could pay the bills—or see the castle and his legacy sold off to the highest bidder.

The sudden discovery of his parents' wedding certificate after so many years smacked of deceit, but no one contested the matter in court. Why should they? They needed Alistair to set the estate to rights if they wanted their yearly sums. Oh, his stepmother had been furious, but her son, Charles, had seemed only relieved. He'd promptly moved to London to carouse and hop from one scandal to another, which meant Alistair himself had to travel down from the north to mop up the mess.

Lady Prescott rapped her fan on the arm of her chair to capture his attention. He lifted a brow in question.

"As I was *saying*, Alistair," she repeated, her lips puckered in the displeasure of finding herself ignored. "The children could belong to *anyone*. How can we be certain Charles even fathered the brats?"

Alistair expelled an exasperated breath. "Take a wee look at their eyes," he grated. "Even *you* cannot deny the Cassilis green." Both children shared the bright, distinct Cassilis green with flecks of blue around the pupils surrounded by a darker rich, deep emerald ring.

Lady Prescott's double chin jiggled in distaste. "Well, the woman was a…" She paused to grimace behind her fan.

"A mere laundress?" Alistair finished for her.

"Yes, I will say it, Alistair. The woman was a low-born laundress." The words burst from her mouth as if she could not hold them back. "Let *her* relations take the mongrel, beggar children in. It's unfitting we should be involved. Our reputation! Charles is a high-born—"

"Drunken sot," Alistair inserted coolly. "A sot refusing to provide for his offspring, and a sot happy to abandon them upon your doorstep so he may carouse on the continent. Good God, woman, can you truly suggest we abandon two wee, motherless children on the streets? Simply because their mother was—heaven forbid—a mere *laundress?*"

His aunt bristled like a hedgehog, her lips pressed so tightly together they turned white. "Alistair, your reputation—"

"Reputation?" he interrupted with a dry chuckle. "I should think my reputation would suffer should I *not* accept responsibility for the poor, motherless children." He held his hands up again, cutting her off. "My decision is made. The lad and lassie travel with me to Culzean, and that's the end of the matter."

Lady Prescott fluttered her fan again, affecting an injured air. "Very well, take them, if you insist, but they hardly need a governess. Let them learn a trade. They're well-born beggars at best and, as such, beneath the notice of polite society."

Alistair lifted his brow a contemptuous notch higher, astonished at the woman's audacity. "I am curious," he murmured. "Those many years ago, after my mother died and I found myself on my father's doorstep...whose idea was it then, to send me to the stables?" He'd arrived at his father's castle, a lad of eight—and had been promptly put to work mucking the stables.

Lady Prescott gave her fan a vicious snap. "We had to protect your father's reputation," she answered through tight lips. "You've no cause to be ungrateful. You're the earl now, aren't you? And this many years later, I am *still* providing assistance. I found eight highly *respected* governesses to care for the two children, Alistair. Eight. Yet, you have refused them all. What am I to do?"

So, if she hadn't sent him to the stables, she'd definitely participated in the notion. He shook his head. Just how hard and withered was her old heart?

"Eight, I repeat." She fanned her cheeks. "Eight."

Alistair folded his arms. Aye, she'd found eight governesses. Eight highly *prejudiced* old biddies who'd fluttered horrified eyelashes upon discovering they'd be educating two children of dubious parentage in a remote Scottish castle near the sea. He'd suffered enough in his youth with such women. He wasn't about to inflict the same kind of pain on two motherless bairns.

A knock on the parlor door prohibited further conversation, and a mob-capped maid entered to whisper hurriedly in his aunt's ear.

"Absolutely *horrifying*," Lady Prescott tutted behind her ever-present fan. "And she is on my *front* doorstep? Whatever is the world coming to? Are you certain I know a Major Atchenson? Why would his daughter come here?"

Alistair tilted his head, curious.

"Yes, my lady." The maid bobbed a curtsey. "Major Atchenson saved your son, young master George, in the war."

Lady Prescott's eyes widened. "Heavens! The very same Major Atchenson? How can that be? Such an ignoble end…" Her fan fluttered furiously. "No, no, I cannot…the gossip alone…no, I can't have her in my household. Show her in, but interrupt me in two minutes, two minutes, mind you. Claim an urgent matter begs my attention and send her away. I'll make certain she doesn't return."

Alistair stared, speechless. Had the woman no shame?

The maid left, then returned with a young woman dressed in a modest, brown, quilted Spencer jacket over a simple high-waist, blue gown, and a straw bonnet in hand.

Alistair's breath caught. She stood just inside the door, a perfect example of feminine beauty, a delicate and pale tragic angel. Her dark-lashed hazel eyes held deep-seated pain and her full downturned lips, betrayed a healthy sense of unease. She'd twisted her gold-tinted, brown locks into a simple bun, but several rebellious strands had escaped and curled around her neck. He dropped his gaze over the soft curve of her jaw.

"Miss Atchenson," his aunt raised her voice in greeting. "Allow me to offer you my sympathies, child. Such a shock, such a shock." She smiled, a most disingenuous smile.

Miss Atchenson dipped into a respectful curtsey to his aunt, then darted an uncertain glance at him. Alistair nodded a polite reply.

Lady Prescott tilted her head his way. "My nephew, Lord Alistair James, Baron Aisla and 11th Earl of Cassilis."

Alistair leveled Lady Cassilis a thin-lipped look. Could her boastful tone possibly be in poorer taste?

"I am told you're seeking *employment*, Miss Atchenson," his aunt addressed the young woman again. The lass brightened and opened her mouth to respond, but the old woman barreled on, "Considering your unfortunate circumstances, I would think it wise for you to look in the country. Perhaps Ireland?"

Miss Atchenson caught her breath. "I...see, my lady."

The maid rushed into the room. "Lady Prescott, a most urgent matter requires your immediate attention."

Alistair folded his arms across his chest. "One urgent matter," he said with a sardonic twist of his lips. "As ordered."

The women in the room froze.

He stepped forward and bowed. "Miss Atchenson, allow me to assist you whilst my dearest aunt of aunts deals with her urgent matter. Our family stands indebted to yours. Without your father's courageous action, my cousin George would no longer grace his mother's dinner table. Is that not true, Lady Prescott?"

His aunt recovered first. With an angry snap of her fan, she scowled at the maid. "The matter will have to wait. I must handle Miss Atchenson's predicament first." She turned to Alistair and added, "My dear boy, pray do not involve yourself. These things are far beneath your attention."

From the expression on her face, it was clear she thought him anything *but* 'dear.' He smiled, a cool, warning smile, and faced the young woman. Miss Atchenson regarded him uneasily. Another victim of the *ton*, to be sure. Well, now that he held a position of some authority, he knew by far the easiest way to provide true assistance to the lass was to face the gossip and rumors head-on.

"Forgive my frankness, Miss Atchenson," he addressed her as kindly as he could, "but might I inquire as to the nature of these 'unfortunate circumstances' my aunt has mentioned?"

Her eyes widened in surprise.

Lady Prescott gasped, horrified. "Heavens, Alistair, how unseemly."

"I mean no disrespect." He summoned a smile. "How can I help otherwise, pray tell?"

Miss Atchenson bravely smiled back. "My father recently met an unexpected and disgraceful end, my lord." Her voice, strong and low, held a musical quality.

For all of her talk of his approach being unseemly, his aunt had no problems jumping in. "Quite shocking." Her eyes lit with the thrill of gossip. "It was in every paper, Alistair, the week before you arrived. *Every* paper. Gambling debts and mismanagement of funds. Thousands of pounds. A decorated major! Such a disgrace. And now? The drinking. There's even talk of frequent visits to houses of ill repute. Why, Lady Witherby says his death was rather too convenient to be an accident and that he, well, you know…" She let her voice trail suggestively away.

Miss Atchenson's eyes flashed, but her lips remained firmly sealed. Aye, the lass obviously wished to defend her father. He found her response and restraint admirable.

Alistair lifted a brow at his aunt's haughty conceit, and couldn't resist saying, "What was that, Lady Prescott? Mismanagement of funds, you say? Rather reminds one of Castle Culzean's former laird, does it not?"

Lady Prescott's jaw dropped open. "Your father had *nothing* in common with—"

"He spent thousands of pounds he did not have," he cut her short. As she sucked in a shocked breath and furiously fanned her reddened cheeks, he eyed the young woman once again. "And what position…" he began, then, a sudden idea crossed his mind. "I assume you read and write, Miss Atchenson?"

His aunt's fan abruptly stilled.

Miss Atchenson's gaze darted quickly between them. "Yes,

my lord."

"You hold some basic knowledge of deportment and polite society? A smattering of French? Can you play at least one song on the pianoforte?"

She hesitated, then nodded.

"Absolutely *not*, Alistair." Lady Prescott pushed to her feet. "You preside over an ancient and noble Scottish house. *Think of your reputation, young sir.*"

Reputation. She couldn't have picked a better word to egg him on. "I need a governess to oversee two wee children at Castle Culzean, clan Cassilis's ancestral home on the Ayrshire coast," he continued smoothly. "A lad and a lassie, raised in London by their mother, a recently deceased laundress and, until now, without proper knowledge of their father's station in life. Were you to secure this position, you would teach them their letters and the ways of polite Society." At this point, the other governesses had flinched. He paused and studied the young woman's reaction.

Miss Atchenson hesitated, then dropped another nervous curtsey. "I am most honored for your consideration, my lord, but I am more suited to the scullery."

Scullery? The word tugged at his heart, reminding him of his mother. "Why not a governess?" he pressed.

She took a deep breath and answered with candor, "I know nothing of raising genteel children, my lord."

Genteel children. His lip curled in a smile. "Aye, you will do quite nicely, Miss Atchenson. The position is yours. I grow weary of London. We leave for Castle Culzean at once. I will send a man with you to gather your things."

Miss Atchenson's eyes widened.

"Have you gone mad?" Lady Prescott struggled to catch her breath.

He eyed the young woman before him. Had he? He didn't really know, but for some odd reason, he didn't truly care.

CHAPTER 3

"What the devil?" Charlotte gave her worn canvas bag another hard yank to dislodge it from the black iron railing that lined the front steps of her old home. The bag came free all at once. She stumbled backward and nearly slid down the icy steps.

"Allow me, Miss Atchenson."

She glanced over her shoulder to see Lord Cassilis's mutton-chop whiskered footman stepping out of the hackney coach he'd hired. The man had been waiting patiently. Not that she'd been long. She had only a worn peach-colored day dress, a thin nightgown, and a hairbrush to pack.

"Thank you, but I am fine," she replied, embarrassed to relinquish a nearly empty bag.

The man nodded and leaned against the coach to wait. Charlotte pulled on her nearly threadbare winter gloves, then turned to inspect the small townhouse for the last time. For the past six years, it had been home—well, where she'd lived, anyway. She'd never felt comfortable in the place. Home, to her, would always be the country cottage of her childhood. She cocked a wry brow at the townhouse, eager to leave it, London, and her problems behind. She'd already exchanged farewells with the butcher's wife. As for the rest of her acquaintances and relatives? They didn't care where she ended up so long as it wasn't on their doorstep. Why tell them anything?

As for Captain Edwards…

She tossed her head and snorted. Let him wonder where she'd vanished off to—not that he would. Nae, she wouldn't think of him again. Why should she? She was free. Free, at last. A thread of excitement wound its way through her at the thought and she smiled for the first time in weeks.

She spun on her heel and headed for the hackney coach with her bag clutched tightly under her arm. She'd no sooner sat down on the scuffed leather carriage seat then the coachman whistled and they were off.

With a deep breath to steady herself, Charlotte leaned her head against the grimy coach window and let London pass unseeing before her eyes. She turned her thoughts to the challenge ahead. Again and again, she heard Lord Cassilis's deep baritone play in her mind. *You will do quite nicely, Miss Atchenson. The position is yours.*

Quite nicely? She bit her lip. She hadn't the slightest notion how to begin. And a smattering of French? Did swearing count? She winced. Why had she nodded? Because she'd been too petrified and desperate to do anything else. At least she *could* play a few songs on the pianoforte—Irish drinking songs. She prayed he wouldn't ask for a concert. She'd only wanted a position as the lowest of scullery maids. She'd never dreamt of becoming a governess to the children of an ancient and noble Scottish house. But given the beggar's power of choice, what could she do?

As for the man himself, he clearly knew no fear. He'd taken on Lady Prescott without a moment's hesitation, a woman none in London dared cross. She shifted uneasily in her seat, unable to shake his image from her mind as he'd stood before the fire, a powerful Scottish lord over six feet tall with thick dark hair and deep green eyes.

"What have you landed yourself in, Charlotte?" she whispered, and blew her truant curls away from her eyes.

She grimaced. She'd have to make do.

All too soon, the hackney rolled to a stop near Lady Prescott's Mayfair address and Charlotte stepped down, her canvas bag close to her side. An impressive barouche waited at the townhouse door, a remarkable conveyance painted an elegant black and emblazoned with the Cassilis coat of arms. Four splendid bays stamped in their gleaming harnesses as several footmen strapped large, iron-banded trunks to the vehicle's rear.

"His lordship awaits inside, Miss Atchenson," the mutton-chop whiskered footman informed her kindly. As she started toward the front door, he caught her arm and quickly added, "The servants' entrance is 'round the back, Miss."

Charlotte checked her step. Ah, yes. As a governess, she followed a different set of rules now. She nodded thanks, then altered course and headed to the proscribed door. A dour-faced maid answered on the second knock and promptly escorted her up the back stairs to a small dormer makeshift nursery with yellow-painted walls, a mattress on the floor, and little else.

Two children stood by the single window overlooking the street below, a young dark-haired boy of approximately nine years of age and a little red-haired, freckle-faced girl of perhaps three. Both shared Lord Cassilis's unusual green eyes and both wore stiff new clothes they obviously found uncomfortable.

Under their watchful gazes, Charlotte took a deep breath and nervously cleared her throat. "Good afternoon, children, I am Miss Charlotte Atchenson, your new governess." She forced her lips into a smile. "And your names are?" She waited.

The children simply stared.

Adding a bit more warmth to her smile, she tried again. "What is your name, young master?"

The boy's dark lashes lowered and his mouth clamped shut —a challenge if ever she'd seen one.

Somewhat startled, Charlotte addressed his sister, "Your name, young mistress?"

The child's big eyes widened even more as she darted behind her brother and grabbed fistfuls of his new wool coat in her tiny hands. The boy stiffened and he held out a protective arm as if to block Charlotte from coming any closer.

"Well, this won't do," Charlotte breathed. They clearly didn't trust her. She'd obviously have to make friends with them first.

At a movement near the door, she glanced over to see Lord Cassilis duck under the lintel to enter the room, the heels of his fine, well-polished black riding-boots a loud click on the attic floor. Rising to his full height, he stood tall in a dark blue waistcoat topped off with a gray silk neck cloth tied with an elegantly careless twist. The folds of his white sleeves and cut of his waistcoat emphasized the breadth of his shoulders. Charlotte realized she was staring and dropped her gaze, only to find her attention diverted to the tight fit of his tailored trousers, where they stretched over his long, lean thighs. Heavens, but she didn't recall him being *quite* so handsome.

"Good afternoon, Miss Atchenson." His deep, Scottish-accented baritone cut into her thoughts.

She snapped her head up. Heat rushed to her cheeks. Had he noticed her gawking? The humor in the dark-lash rimmed, green eyes answered a resounding 'yes'. The chiseled lips crooked into a sensual curl above the dimpled chin.

Horrified, she fumbled a belated curtsey. "Good afternoon, my lord."

"I see you have met your charges." He strode forward to join her.

"Yes, my lord," she croaked.

Charlotte turned to the children, instead, and noted their solemn, shuttered expressions. The little girl still huddled behind her brother's protective arm. Ah, yes. Their names.

She nodded at Lord Cassilis, her focus on his chest, and asked, "Might I know their names, my lord?"

Silence met her request.

When it became apparent he wouldn't answer, she dared a glance at his face, only to see him surveying the children with a mystified expression.

He slanted a smile her way with a graceful incline of his head, and announced, "Children, this is your governess, Miss Atchenson. Step forward and tell her your names."

They didn't budge, nor did they speak.

He waited a moment, then shrugged. "Well then, there you have it." He gave a dry humph of a laugh and shook his head in some private joke. Turning to her, he added, "We leave at once, Miss Atchenson. See the lad and lassie settled in the carriage, will you? And be quick. We are late."

Charlotte frowned, confused. Their names? Did the man not know them? Or was it some strange sort of game? She faced her young charges once again, and mustered her brightest smile. "Come now, children, let's go to the carriage, shall we?"

To her delight, the little girl smiled back and took a timid step forward. But her brother, with a single, large step, blocked her way, eyes flashing outright defiance. Charlotte blinked, startled at the intensity of his reaction.

"You're welcome to stay, lad," Lord Cassilis calmly remarked over her shoulder. "I'm certain Lady Prescott will find you pleasant enough company."

The words had a rousing effect. The boy seized his sister's

wrist and pulled her toward the door. Charlotte started forward, but he ran with his sister down the stairs before Charlotte reached the first step. A deep chuckle rumbled through Lord Cassilis's chest as he stepped up behind her.

"My lord." Charlotte raised a brow. "Please, sir," she smoothed her suddenly sweating palms over her skirt. "Might I know their names?"

His eyes twinkled as he bent close and whispered in her ear, "I confess, my dear Miss Atchenson, I haven't the faintest notion of what they might be."

His breath warmed her ear. She took a startled step back.

His lips quirked in a devilish grin. "But please do not let them know, aye? Especially the lad." He spun on his heel and strode down the hallway.

Charlotte stared in astonishment. What manner of man failed to know the names of his own children? And the boy? She'd recognized the raw emotion under that defiance. She'd seen it often enough in the mirror, staring back at her from within her own eyes. Anger. *Deep* anger. She'd do well to stay on her toes.

"What a fine kettle of fish you've landed yourself in," she groused, then marched down the stairs after them.

Charlotte caught up with the children in the foyer. Lady Prescott wasn't there to bid adieu, but the staff had formed a respectful line leading to the open door. They bowed and curtsied their farewells as Lord Cassilis acknowledged each one on his walk toward the door. Finally, he reached the end of the line where the butler waited, holding a dark wool overcoat and a black silk top hat.

"Safe travels, my lord," the butler spoke in soft, polite tones, as he handed Lord Cassilis the hat and coat.

With a crisp nod, Lord Cassilis swirled the great overcoat over his broad shoulders and clapped the hat on his head, then stepped out the front door.

Charlotte took it as her cue to follow and shooed the children forward, but this time, the staff responded with only chill, silent stares and, by the time they'd reached the end of the line, the butler had long gone. Affronted on the children's behalf, she hurried them out the door and down the steps.

"Pay the judgmental creatures no heed," she advised as she marched them down the walk to the waiting barouche.

"We will not be traveling far, milord," the coachman was saying to Lord Cassilis as they neared. "I fear it will snow."

Charlotte glanced at the line of dark clouds massed on the northern horizon. Indeed, it did look like snow, but the prospect of returning to Lady Prescott's oppressive household looked even worse.

Apparently, Lord Cassilis felt the same. "If we get no farther than a mile from this house, I will dance with joy." He stepped back and waved Charlotte and the children to the carriage.

The mutton-chop whiskered footman helped the children into the coach. When he grasped Charlotte's hand, she ducked as she entered, then paused. Double-stitched, quilted, black leather lined every inch of the luxurious interior. Ornate brass oil lamps hung on either side of the door. The polished plate glass windows rested in gilded frames with crimson velvet curtains held back in gold-tasseled loops. The seats, soft and plump, with fleece-lined lap blankets, begged to be used. A finely woven carpet covered the floor.

"Miss Atchenson?"

Charlotte startled at Lord Cassilis's voice so near her elbow. She turned and plopped down on the seat beside the little girl. From the corner of her eye, she glimpsed Lord Cassilis's large frame as he grasped the handle. She jerked her gaze aside and spotted a folded blanket on the seat beside the boy.

Crossing her fingers he would listen, she pointed at the blanket. "Hand me the blanket, sweetheart, and I shall tuck it around you and your sister for our journey."

To her relief, he obeyed, perhaps as eager to leave Lady Prescott's domain as she was herself. She quickly shook out the blanket and spread it over their legs. She'd just tucked it around them when the carriage dipped under Lord Cassilis's weight.

He ducked as he entered the small space and removed his hat as he took the seat opposite them. The door closed with a click and he rapped sharply on the window to signal the coachman their readiness to leave. Hat on his lap, he settled back and stretched his long legs to the side. With a long sigh of apparent relief, he closed his eyes.

The barouche lurched forward and Charlotte caught sight of the footmen, mounted on fine geldings and dressed in warm coats and scarves against the bitter winter air, before they disappeared behind the carriage. As the clip-clop of the horses' hooves and the jingle of harnesses filled the air, Charlotte heaved a deep breath of relief. It was really happening. She was leaving London. At last. She glanced at the children and read an excitement in their eyes that mirrored her own.

She smiled.

It was the wrong move. The boy responded with a dark scowl and deliberately turned his bony shoulders away to ignore her. Charlotte suppressed a snort. Well, she'd outwit the little trouble-causer. Give her time. Still, it would be helpful to know what had made him so distrustful. Perhaps Lord Cassilis had taken too long in accepting his responsibility?

From the corner of her eye, she studied the man. Heavens, he was a handsome devil. The kind of man who could charm birds right out of the trees. The children's mother had likely found him irresistible. But he had to be a cad...a man *should* know the names of his own children. Her mouth twisted in disapproval.

Almost as if sensing the subject of her thoughts, the dark ruffled line of his lashes fluttered. Charlotte yanked her gaze to the window. Shame washed over her. She, of all people, had no cause to judge. She could only be grateful. After all, the man had basically plucked her off the streets and made her a governess...a role for which she was scarcely qualified. She winced. Well, she could read and write. Pianoforte? Eh, maybe she could stay ahead of her pupil. But French? Melting back in her seat, she scavenged her memories for every French word she might have heard, wondering how many a smattering made.

The barouche threaded its way through north through London, and when Charlotte looked at the children again, she found them fast asleep, mouths slack. She studied their thin, pinched faces. Poor motherless mites. They probably felt much like herself, lost and overwhelmed.

A glance at Lord Cassilis revealed he'd fallen asleep as well. She had to admit. Something about him drew her eye. The firmness of his lips? The sensual line of his jaw? Oh, he was quite attractive. If he looked at her with even a hint of passion in those striking eyes, could she resist? Heat flooded her cheeks. She hastily forced her gaze back out the window and schooled her thoughts into the task that lay ahead as governess.

The carriage rolled on. Slowly, they left London behind, always heading north, until the sun sank below the horizon and darkness fell. The footmen took the lead with bright torches and lanterns to light the way along the forested road. The way turned rough. The carriage jolted and creaked along, rocking her body to the uneven rhythm.

Still, the children and Lord Cassilis slept.

Snow began to fall. The footmen's torches illuminated the large, feathery flakes that drifted down from the canopy of darkness above. Charlotte pressed her cheek against the window and trailed a finger down the plate glass, dreamily following the snowflakes' lazy descent.

She abruptly became aware of being watched and glanced

over her shoulder. Lord Cassilis's green eyes glittered against the faint flicker of the exterior torchlight. She froze, heart beating like a drum as their gazes locked. Long seconds passed before his eyes slid away. Her cheeks heated and she busied herself with adjusting the children's blanket when the distinct odor of urine unexpectedly wafted up to her. Frowning, she lifted a corner of the fleece for a closer inspection. The odor blasted her nostrils. She squinted until she discerned a dark, wet patch on the little girl's dress.

"My lord." She cleared her throat. "We must stop the carriage."

The children awoke with a start.

Lord Cassilis queried softly, "Why must we do so, Miss Atchenson?"

Charlotte hesitated. How did one tell a peer of the realm that his daughter had wet her petticoat? "A necessity. A necessity of nature, sir."

"A necessity of nature?" he repeated.

She sent him an exasperated look. What did the man *expect* when traveling with children? Yes, he didn't know their names, but did that mean he knew *nothing* of their care?

Understanding dawned on his handsome face. "Ah, I see." He shrugged. "But the deed is already done, is it not? Can't... she..." His voice trailed off when Charlotte stared in shock and he heaved a sigh, half-annoyed, half-amused. "Very well, then."

He gave the window a solid rap.

The carriage rolled to a stop.

A footman opened the door and torchlight filled the interior. Charlotte took the girl by the hand and addressed her employer once again, "I will need fresh clothes, my lord."

His inscrutable gaze raked her from head to toe. "Very well," he granted, then addressed the footman, "Ye heard her, I'm sure? Untie the children's trunk."

A little flustered, Charlotte stepped down from the carriage into ankle-deep snow with both children close behind. It didn't take long to search through their trunk. It was practically empty. Charlotte pulled out the only other dress inside—a thin, patched pink fabric adorned with a limp, bedraggled ribbon— and held it up in the torchlight.

"Is this all you have?" she asked, surprised.

Both children nodded.

"Well then, it must do." She nodded her thanks to the footman, then escorted the little girl to the nearest tree. The girl's brother followed and Charlotte hid a smile when he stood guard while she and the girl stepped out of sight behind the trunk.

In minutes, they were back inside the carriage, the children rosy-cheeked and shivering. Someone had lit the interior brass lamps during the wait. Charlotte bundled the children back under their blanket and wondered if their feet were as cold and wet as hers. Flickering light caught the gilded windows and the silver buttons of Lord Cassilis's fine overcoat. The contrast to the child's worn dress couldn't be sharper.

Charlotte settled back beside the lass and couldn't stop herself from saying, "My lord, your children are in dire need of clothes."

Surprise shone in his eyes. His chiseled lips parted as if to reply, then his gaze fell on the children. An awkward moment of silence passed before he said in a mild voice, "Then see to it, Miss Atchenson."

She nodded, pleased.

A ghost of a smile curved his lips. "If you are satisfied, may we leave?"

Her stomach fluttered at the smoky timber of his voice. She managed a prim, "Yes, my lord. As it pleases you."

Once again, he rapped on the plate glass window.

Silence returned. The carriage lumbered on. And this time, lulled by the vehicle's gentle sway, Charlotte fell asleep.

"Miss Atchenson," a man's deep voice intruded upon her dreams. "Miss Atchenson, we've arrived."

Charlotte frowned. "Go away." She melted deeper into the corner, seeking a more comfortable position.

"Miss Atchenson," the deep voice insisted with a distinct note of humor. "We have arrived."

This time, someone shook her shoulder.

"Devil take you, sirrah. Can you not see I am trying to sleep?" She slapped at the fingers that gently gripped her arm. Realization pierced the haze of her thoughts and she froze. She'd fallen asleep. *Even worse, had she just sworn at her employer?*

Charlotte jumped to her feet and collided with the solid, muscled wall of Lord Cassilis's chest. He grunted and chuckled a, "Ho, lass," as he fell back under her momentum. His hands fell about her waist as he landed on the opposite seat and she tumbled into his lap.

Heart pounding, Charlotte stared up into his green eyes.

His mouth twitched in humor. "That will teach me not to wake you from a sound sleep, eh, lass?"

Charlotte swallowed. His eyes shifted to her throat. Something primal leapt to life in his green eyes. A charged tension ignited between them. Slowly, he released her, trailing a hand down her hip before she was able to shove off his thighs.

She plopped onto the opposite seat and managed a subdued, "Pardon me, my lord."

"We will lodge here for the night, Miss Atchenson," he said, quite unruffled, and rose to exit through the carriage door.

Embarrassment washed over her. She hadn't noticed the open door. Had everyone witnessed their inappropriate encounter? To her dismay, Lord Cassilis extended a hand into the carriage to help her down. He nodded and her gaze caught on his dimpled chin. She placed her hand in his. As his large fingers swallowed hers, she tried her best to ignore the shiver of attraction. Heavens, what *was* it about the man?

She touched down on the ground and he released her. He stood for a moment, eyes intent on her face, then touched his fingertip to the brim of his hat, and moved to join the footmen untying the trunks at the back.

Charlotte caught sight of the children, huddled together a few feet away. She hurried to their side and took a moment to study her surroundings as Lord Cassilis directed the unloading of the luggage. The carriage stood in front of a tidy stone inn at the edge of a small village as picturesque as a painting. Pine trees surrounded a courtyard blanketed with snow, and an oil lantern swayed on a lamp-post by the door. The inn's diamond-paned, leaded windows twinkled with lights that made her think of a hot meal and a warm bed.

A wave of exhaustion washed over her as she stretched her hands toward the children. "Let's go, shall we?"

They didn't hold her hands, but they followed her properly enough, perhaps enticed by thoughts of a hot meal and a bed themselves. Whatever the reason, she felt grateful. She hadn't strength enough to engage in a new clash of wills.

She'd no sooner bustled them inside the inn than Lord Cassilis joined them with his black silk hat tucked under his arm. With a nod for her to wait, he crossed the small reception area in three long strides and, in minutes, the short, wiry innkeeper slid two large skeleton keys on brass rings across the counter.

Looping the keys over his thumb, Lord Cassilis yawned and waved for them to follow. He led them through a maze of narrow, twisting passages.

Charlotte hurried behind him, and tried her best to ignore the muscled thighs of the man she'd sat on in the carriage. She found herself relieved in more ways than one when he finally paused before a door and fitted a key into the lock.

The lock tuned with a click, then he stood aside and said, "This is where you'll stay with the children."

With a quick but tired nod, Charlotte shepherded the children into the room. It was a pleasant enough place with one large bed located against the far wall and another placed near the window. A table stood before a fire that crackled in an iron grate, and a rose-colored china basin stood in one corner.

"Your supper and luggage will arrive shortly," Lord Cassilis announced. "I bid you good night."

Charlotte turned and bobbed a quick curtsey. "Good night, my lord," she replied. He grasped the doorknob to pull the door closed and she recalled that, as a governess, she held the responsibility to teach her charges the ways of polite society. Clapping her hands, she ordered as kindly as she could, "Bid your father good night, children."

They stared at her with unblinking eyes.

The little devils. Of course, she should have *known* they'd resist. The tips of her ears warmed with embarrassment, but she tossed a glance over her shoulder to gauge Lord Cassilis's reaction as the door softly clicked shut. Her jaw dropped open.

"Polite society?" she snorted under her breath. The man *clearly* stood in need of a governess himself.

She pulled off her gloves one finger at a time and bade the children wash their faces and hands. She'd just gotten her gloves off when a knock rattled the door. Charlotte opened the door and the footmen entered with the luggage, followed by a maid with a large tray of covered dishes. Surprisingly, this time, the children listened when Charlotte instructed them to sit at the table. Most likely, their obedience had everything to do with the food rather than her asking.

Whatever the case, in short order, they sat down at a table set with parsnip and savory roast pork pie, a dish of chestnuts, and a flavorsome boiled cod and oyster-sauce casserole. It was a silent but tasty meal. The children ate quickly and with better manners than she'd expected but, at the end of the meal, the little girl yawned, nearly falling asleep at the table.

Charlotte rose, picked up the small dish of chestnuts, and held it out to the boy. "Why don't you teach your sister how to roast these in the fire? I'll tidy up a bit and find your bedclothes."

He glowered but, to her delight, snatched the dish and pulled his sister to the coals glowing in the grate.

Charlotte smiled. At least, he hadn't refused her suggestion outright. With a sigh, she went to the children's trunk. She unclasped the brass locks and opened the lid, only to be greeted by the rank stench of the little girl's soiled dress. She groaned inwardly. She'd forgotten all about the thing.

A burst of giggles from the fireplace caught her attention and she glanced back. The children relaxed on their stomachs before the fire. She smiled, turned back to the dress, shook it out, and held it up for inspection. It was well-made and very new—a much more fitting dress for the daughter of an earl than the worn thing she wore now. Damnation. She couldn't see a way around it. Lord Cassilis had a reputation to uphold. She would have to wash the dress and dry it before the fire.

A chestnut cracked and the giggles grew louder.

Charlotte set the soiled dress aside, then dug deeper in the chest in search of bedclothes. After a moment, she realized there weren't any. She'd have to see to the children's wardrobe at once and—

An eye-burning and acrid stench crossed her nostrils. Charlotte jumped to her feet and whirled. Thick, black smoke billowed from the grate. Her heart leapt to a gallop. She dashed to the hearth and yanked the children back, then grabbed the poker and stabbed the fire, sending a fresh surge of smoke, along with sparks, out into the room.

"Did you put something in there?" she choked out the question.

Neither child answered, but she hadn't expected them to. Coughing, she covered her nose with her arm and poked the fire again in an effort to identify the source of the smoke. A sudden tower of flames ignited, clearing the smoke just enough to reveal the root cause.

Charlotte could only stare at Lord Cassilis's black silk top hat going up in flames.

"Damnation!" she swore.

The boy grinned, green eyes alight.

Charlotte planted her hands on her hips. "How could you do this?" Another black cloud of smoke gusted over her. She coughed and jabbed a finger at the burning hat. "I understand you resent your father, but he is making amends *now*, is he not? And whatever *has* happened, you simply *cannot* burn hats in the fire willy-nilly, young man."

The mirth died on the boy's face. Their gazes locked in a clash of wills. Charlotte stared. Three heartbeats passed before he looked away. Still irritated, Charlotte blew hair from her face, then strode to the window and shoved it open. She faced the young miscreants once again.

"To bed, the both of you." She cocked a censorious brow at the boy and added, "I will inform you of your punishment in the morning, young sir, and just *how* you will confess to your father what happened to his fine hat."

He glared, but turned, shoulders slumped, and shuffled to the bed. He climbed beneath the blankets, his little sister scrambling in close behind him. As they burrowed beneath the covers, Charlotte returned to the window to fan more smoke out of the room. Thank *heavens*, they hadn't burnt the place down. She'd been quite lucky. In the future, she'd do well to keep a *much* closer eye on the mischief-makers. And the hat? She didn't relish the thought of informing Lord Cassilis she'd let his son burn his hat under her very nose. *Deuce take it.* How and when had the child *filched* the thing? Hadn't it been on his father's head?

When the room had sufficiently cleared and she could breathe easily once again, she closed the window all but a crack and returned to the bed to peer down at her charges. To her relief, they'd both fallen asleep. She heaved a long sigh through her nose and pulled the covers up under their chins. Poor mites—mischievous mites. Yes, she pitied them, but she couldn't let them rule the roost. Tomorrow, she'd wring their names out of them or dub them with names of her own choosing.

She tidied the room, confident the children's slow, deep breathing signaled they still slept, grabbed the soiled dress and slipped away in search of soap and water. It was late, the guests had already retired along with most of the help, but she found an aproned matron in the kitchen who kindly lent her a bar of lye soap and a bucket of hot water.

In short order, she had the dress scrubbed and wrung dry and started back to her room, eyes burning with exhaustion. After she hung the dress before the fire, she could hop into bed. She couldn't wait. It had been a long, trying day. At her door, she smothered a yawn, twisted the knob, and gave the door a solid shove.

It didn't move.

Charlotte blinked and frowned. A quick glance confirmed she did, indeed, stand in front of the correct door. She rattled the knob again.

Giggles emanated from the room. Her heart sank.

Damnation. They *hadn't* been asleep, after all. *They'd locked her out.*

"Open the door at once," she hissed.

Small footsteps ran to the door and for a single relieved moment, she thought they'd listen.

"Nae," came the giggling reply, then the feet scampered away.

Well, at least the boy could talk. Why, oh, why, hadn't she remembered to take the key? She already knew she couldn't trust the children. Frustrated, she banged her forehead softly against the door before making up her mind. Fine. She'd have to outwit the scoundrels. She could ask the innkeeper if he had another key. But that required waking the man and making a scene—a scene that Lord Cassilis would no doubt find out about tomorrow. Surely, there had to be another way. She couldn't let him discover his children had outfoxed her on the very first night.

An idea struck. *The window.* She'd left it open. Charlotte flew down the maze of passages, mentally mapping them as she went along. The inn had been built in a haphazard fashion over the years, but finally, she found a door leading outside. Carefully, she lifted the latch, then stepped out into the night.

The clouds had retreated from the sky and exposed a bright moon that provided ample illumination as she picked her way through the snow. Wind ruffled her hair. The snow had already begun to melt. Several clumps slid into the heel of her shoes. Charlotte grimaced. She detested wet feet. With her mood rapidly deteriorating, she traced her way back to her room. It took longer than expected. She'd almost given up when she found it, a window with roughly the same view and still ajar.

"You can't defeat *me*, young sir," she muttered. "So, you don't have a name, do you? Then I'll take care of *that*. I'll think of the *perfect* one for you."

She stomped to the window, pulled it open, tossed the wet dress inside, and threw a leg over the ledge. The rip of cloth, caused her to freeze and glance back. Her dress had snagged on a nail.

"Deuce take it," she grumbled. Now she'd have to mend her dress as well. Would the night *ever* end? She reached back and carefully lifted her dress free.

The next moment, a pair of strong hands grabbed her about

the waist and yanked her inside. She landed against a broad, well-defined, and very bare chest. She opened her mouth, but the scream died on her lips as a shaft of moonlight fell upon her assailant. Charlotte recognized the sensual jawline, and lifted her gaze to the green eyes that stared down at her.

Lord Alistair Cassilis.

CHAPTER 4

ALISTAIR PACED THE LENGTH OF HIS ROOM, RESTLESS AND unbearably hot. The overly eager-to-please innkeeper had stoked the fire beyond what he could withstand—or at least, that was the prevailing theory. He'd promptly divested himself of his waistcoat. His loose-linen shirt had followed. It hadn't helped. He'd finally cracked open the window for a breath of fresh, cold air, and stood there for a time, letting his thoughts wander where they really wished to go: Miss Charlotte Atchenson.

He'd made the most dreadful mistake in hiring her.

The lass could bring him to his knees. He'd already seen enough flashes of that lively, fierce spirit, simmering just below the surface, to intrigue him. And her warm, hazel eyes? So very expressive. Her lips, so very kissable. When he'd awakened her in the carriage, she'd jumped straight into his arms. Aye, he'd been so distracted by those so very kissable lips he'd struggled to let her go.

Suddenly aware of himself grinning like a fool, he frowned and stepped back from the window. He expelled a deep breath, uncertain at the intensity of his attraction to her. Most likely, he'd been so distracted with estate affairs, he had simply forgone female company for far too long. What else could it be? She provoked an unusually strong response deep within him, something he couldn't recall experiencing the like of before.

Never had he met a woman who could make his blood boil in the space of a single day. He hadn't thought such an attraction possible. It most likely wasn't. His reaction had to be due to something else. But whatever the cause, he had two weeks yet to go before they reached Culzean Castle. The thought concerned him. If the strength of the attraction continued, traveling in such close quarters would be nothing short of a nightmare.

A scratching sound at the window intruded on his thoughts and he looked over to see fingers curling around the frame. The window began to lift. He frowned. A drunkard? A mischief maker? He took three long strides, then caught sight of her face and the soft brown curls, and halted. It couldn't be. But it was. The governess, Charlotte. He watched, astonished, as she tossed a wet rag onto the floor and then swung one leg over the window ledge. Her skirt rode up to expose a slender, elegant leg. He raked his gaze over the exposed flesh. Such a lovely leg.

Her skirt caught on something outside the window. "Deuce take it," she swore, and yanked to free her dress.

Alistair grasped her slender waist and yanked her inside. She fell against him hard enough to cause him to stumble back a few paces. He caught himself. Her head snapped up and she gave a small gasp that sent a message directly to his manhood. He swallowed, startled how swiftly his body responded to her softness and the spill of her hair against his bare skin. By Jove, a man wasn't safe removing his shirt in the privacy of his own bedchambers.

Charlotte's jaw dropped open in shock. "My lord! *Whatever are you doing here?*"

Alistair released her, then hurriedly retrieved his linen shirt even as a wicked grin of amusement curled his lips. Shrugging into his shirt-sleeves, he faced her, then began fastening the buttons.

"Why, Miss Atchenson, where else did you expect me to be?"

Her eyes grew round. "The children? Where are the children?"

Her alarmed expression startled him. Alistair paused in buttoning his shirt. "They should be asleep in their room."

Her brows dove downward and she cast a quick glance around the room. Before he could say more, her cheeks colored with a blush and the truth hit him. She had thought this room was theirs.

"*Sacre-bleu*," she exclaimed.

Alistair blinked, then the devil possessed him, and he said, "Pray tell, Miss Atchenson, do you make a habit of wandering in the snow and entering through strange windows in the dead of night?"

She scooped up the wet rag and displayed what he realized was a little girl's dress. "I had to wash this, my lord. Pardon the intrusion. I didn't mean to disturb you. If you'll excuse me, I will go now."

She turned and took a step toward the window, but he caught her by the wrist. He merely meant to offer the use of the door, but the moment his skin touched hers, an exquisite wave of torment left him struggling for air like a drowning man. She stared up at him. What man could resist a woman so obviously unaware of her effect on him?

Reluctantly, he released her and let his hand fall to his side. "The hellion locked you out, didn't he?"

Uncertainty shone in her eyes, then he smiled. She shook her head and an answering grin teased the corner of her mouth. His gaze fixed on her soft, pink lips.

"It's of no concern, my lord," she said. "Your children do not yet know me."

Your children. The words hit like a bucket of cold water. Och, she thought him a wayward father, a cad who didn't even know the names of his own offspring. He'd meant to correct her in the carriage, but the lad's expression had struck him to the quick. He knew that look, the exact same expression he'd worn himself at precisely that age and for entirely the same reason. An angry—yet hopeful—expression. Let the lad believe him to be the man responsible for his suffering. That was preferable to letting his anger fester and rot his soul as he searched for his father behind every man's face. In the meantime, if the world thought Alistair a wayward, scoundrel of a man—then so be it.

Still, he couldn't let the children run wild. "The lad and lassie should treat their governess with respect." He turned and started toward the door.

"My lord." Charlotte dashed forward and laid a restraining hand on his arm. "They are simply being children."

He paused and peered down at her. Did she think him a violent man? "And?" He noticed her touch and dropped his gaze to her fingers still resting on his arm.

Her eyes snapped to his arm and she snatched her hand back. "They must learn to trust me," she said.

As he would have her trust him. Might she trust him one day? He shook off the thought and started forward again. "Undoubtedly, you will earn their trust, but I must teach them discipline." Something their ne'er-do-well father should have done long ago.

Moments later, he stood before her door, the lady beside him. Alistair raised a hand to knock, then paused. Might it be possible…? He grasped the knob and twisted.

The knob turned and the door swung back easily.

Charlotte drew in a sharp breath. "It was locked, my lord. I swear it."

He leaned into the room. The children lay in bed, asleep—or feigning it well enough. He snorted. Aye, his nephew was a crafty lad. He'd have to find other ways to put that cunning mind to use.

"I…excuse the intrusion, my lord," Charlotte mumbled.

Alistair looked down at her and smiled. "Not at all, Miss Atchenson. I shall expect you and the children in the parlor for breakfast. We will leave directly after. Good evening."

He left her there, curtsying in the doorway, and strode back to his room. After that interesting interlude, sleep would not come easy.

"BLAST IT! WHERE COULD IT BE?" ALISTAIR SWORE.

He'd just fastened the last silver cuff-link to his shirt, then inspected his reflection in the mirror, taking in the simple white knotted neck cloth, the superbly tailored waistcoat of light blue brocade, and the freshly polished boots. Satisfied, he'd glanced over at the bed, where his great overcoat lay freshly brushed. All was as it should be—except he had no hat.

A thorough search of his room by him and his footman proved fruitless. At home on his ancestral lands, he rarely bothered with such fripperies as hats. The raging sea winds that battered the Ayrshire coast made wearing them impossible. However, in England, a man of his station must wear a hat —reluctantly or not. Alistair barked at the footman to find the pesky thing, then he headed for the breakfast parlor.

Brow furrowed, he pulled the gold filigree pocket watch from his front pocket and squinted at the face. Eight o'clock. The night had been dreadful—as expected. He hadn't slept a wink. He'd tried, but his thoughts always circled back to Charlotte, starting with her arrival in Lady Prescott's home, through the carriage ride, and ending with her lovely leg thrown across his window sill.

With the smell of ham, eggs and blessed coffee calling him like a siren, he hurried around the hallway corner and nearly ran straight into the subject of his thoughts. Charlotte walked with the children toward the breakfast parlor door.

He ducked back behind the corner as she said, "I have thought of a happy solution to our problem, young master." Alistair peeked around the corner as she adjusted the back of the boy's collar. "Since you will not share your name, I shall bless you with a name of my own."

Alistair grinned. So, the lad still tortured his governess, did he? He had to admire the boy's pluck.

"I've considered the matter quite carefully." She straightened the wee lassie's hair ribbon. "And I have chosen a lovely name, so very lovely, indeed."

Alistair noted the provocative sway of Charlotte's slender hips. Already, several wavy strands of her hair had escaped the confines of its prim bun to curl around the tempting curve of her neck.

Charlotte lifted a finger in the air like a sword and touched the boy's shoulders as if she were knighting him. Alistair couldn't help but admire the way the soft folds of her dress outlined her breasts as she gestured and announced in a solemn voice, "I dub thee, Abigail."

Alistair tore his eyes from her breasts.

The boy's mouth dropped open. "That's a *girl's* name!"

Charlotte placed her hand over her heart and feigned surprise. "Ah, so you *can* speak? How pleasant it is to hear your voice this fine morn, sweet Abigail."

"'Tis not my name," the boy insisted.

Ignoring his sullen response, Charlotte herded them

through the breakfast parlor door, saying, "Come, dear Abigail. Let us not be late."

Alistair straightened his waistcoat and stepped forward to join them, when a familiar voice hailed him from behind, "What the devil? Do my eyes deceive me?"

He glanced back to see his friend, Sir Nicholas Hunter Blair, 4th Baronet of Dunskey, striding down the hall toward him. Standing over six feet tall, the baronet radiated a graceful masculinity and aristocratic breeding not only with his striking patrician cheekbones and strong noble jaw, but his cunning wit and keen eye as well, an eye that missed little—save where women were involved. Alistair often wondered if the women played him for a fool, or if he simply enjoyed letting them play the game.

Nicholas reached him and Alistair grasped the man's shoulder. "That I've lived to see the day you grace a humble village inn instead of a fashionable London hotel. What brings you here, lad?"

Nicholas' ice-blue eyes lit with a smile. "Why, *you* do, my dear fellow." He nodded his raven head toward the breakfast parlor door. "That and a good, old-fashioned breakfast."

Alistair snorted in disbelief. "Since when have you ever risen before noon? I'd wager you've yet to fall asleep."

"And I must confess you are right," the baronet admitted with an unrepentant grin. "Truth is, I stand in need of your help, but I'm rather curious, as well, as to why you abandoned Culzean for London this time of year, which forced me to chase you hither and yon, all over the country?"

"What is the only reason that ever brings me here?" Alistair asked.

Nicholas clucked his tongue. "What has Charles done *this* time?"

Alistair heaved a long sigh and raked his fingers through his hair. "It's a long tale, my friend. Let's find a private place to speak, aye?" He couldn't chance the children overhearing.

They strode to the parlor door, and Alistair stopped and peered inside. It was a small room, pleasant enough, with windows that overlooked the courtyard, and a sideboard laden with a variety of muffins, cakes, and eggs. The children squirmed impatiently at the large oak table in the center of the room, clearly displeased with having to wait, as Charlotte hovered behind the little girl, attempting yet again to tie a ribbon in her unruly red locks.

He meant to tell them not to wait, that he'd eat elsewhere, but Charlotte chose that moment to bite her lip in concentration and he found himself wondering just how those soft, pink lips would taste.

"Where did he find *her?*" Nicholas' whispered words were followed by a long, low whistle.

At the sound, Charlotte and the children glanced up.

"Please, eat." Alistair nodded at the sideboard. "I have a matter to attend. There's no need to wait."

As Charlotte bobbed a curtsey, he spun on his heel, brusquely waving his friend to follow.

"She's a bit out of his league, is she not?" Nicholas began.

"No' her," Alistair interrupted, irritated. After trying a few doors, he found a small, empty sitting room with two shabby velvet chairs and a small table, both placed before a fire long grown cold. No sooner had the door closed behind them, he added, "It's the children, Nicholas. Charles' children. Their mother died and he could only bother himself to have them dumped on Lady Prescott's doorstep before vanishing off to the continent in search of new pleasures."

"Ah, my dear fellow, I find myself no longer interested in Charles' latest escapade."

Alistair didn't like the lusty gleam that lit Nicholas' ice-blue eyes.

"Who is she?" Nicholas demanded.

Alistair moved to a nearby chair and folded his arms over the back. Nicholas' well-deserved reputation as a rake made him an undesirable candidate to spend time with Charlotte.

"No one you need know," Alistair said.

The man's keen eyes narrowed in the instant before he crossed the room. He seated himself in the chair beside Alistair and stretched his long legs as he inspected Alistair from head to toe.

"A bit defensive, are you? I would say, even possessive."

"She is no concern of yours," Alistair replied.

"Come, come," his friend pressed with a charming smile. "'Tis not like you to be defensive over a lass, Alistair. Is she—"

"Leave it be," Alistair cut him short. "I am not jesting, lad."

The man studied him for a moment, then a slow smile spread over his face. "Then let us speak of other matters." He withdrew a coin from his waistcoat pocket and began flipping it in the air. "I have been looking for you."

"Why, when surely a letter would do?"

"With mail coaches bogged down by the snow and roads impassable, it's no wonder you haven't gotten them. I sent three. But then, perhaps Lady Prescott lost them for you?" He snorted. "There is matter of great delicacy, best dealt with in person, as it requires I take you into my confidence and provide an explanation."

"Explanation?" Alistair echoed, now suspicious.

Nicholas widened his grin. "An explanation as to why you'll arrive at Culzean to find my guests most likely already there for a most delightful house party."

It took a moment for the words to sink in. "Guests? Pray tell, what house party is this?"

"Why, yours, my dear fellow," Nicholas answered smoothly. "I couldn't invite her to Dunskey without a misunderstanding. I have only just met the lass."

Alistair groaned. "You invited your lover to Culzean?"

"Nae, not lover. Not yet. She misunderstood. She's bringing *chaperones*. Her cousin, some captain, who will no doubt cause problems." He wrinkled his nose in distaste. Then, with a mischievous grin, he leaned forward. "Perhaps I should demonstrate the pain of the word, aye? Now that I find you here at an inn with a delightful...unless, of course, you're not fancying her in that way..." He let his voice trail off.

Alistair locked gazes with him. "She is not to be trifled with, Nicholas."

A tense silence drew out between them.

After a moment, Nicholas relaxed back into his chair. "Then I fancy I will enjoy watching."

"Why Culzean?" Alistair set the conversation back on track. "I fail to—"

"It's a bit of a situation, if you must know," Nicholas cut in. "And really, why let that grand castle of yours simply rot? You can host a house party with far greater ease than I can. Having it all at Culzean is quite the tidy solution."

"For who?" Alistair grated, but then his attention snagged on the word 'all'. He lifted a brow. "Having it *all* at Culzean?"

Nicholas laughed. "We've talked about this before," he replied, dancing around the issue.

An indirect answer from Nicholas didn't bode well—especially where women were involved. "Say it, Nicholas," Alistair ordered. "Have done."

"It's nothing, really. Just a few guests for a month or so. The rest won't even arrive until the, uh, spring ball."

There it was. The dark, treacherous water lurking under the fresh hay. "Spring ball?" Alistair queried in a low, dangerous voice.

Nicholas shrugged, unperturbed. "A celebration of completing Culzean's renovation. What worthier cause than that? And may I remind you, that *you* owe *me*." He stressed the words with a lazy grin.

"How so?"

"That card game last summer, at the Gordon's wedding party."

Alistair didn't break his stare. "Do you refer to the card game...that *I* won?"

You? Nicholas mouthed the word, lifting both brows as if in surprise.

Alistair studied him in an attempt to gauge whether or not his response was genuine. With his consummate acting skills, it was often difficult to tell.

The baronet clapped his palm to his forehead in embarrassment and grinned his widest yet. "Did *you* win, Alistair?" he asked in astonishment. "Zounds, you *did*, didn't you? What a merry blunder. I was certain you stood in my debt. I fear it's too late to change plans now. I've contrived to make a right jolly celebration of it."

Alistair opened his mouth, prepared to share his own opinion on that score when Nicholas raised a staying hand. "But before we discuss it further, perhaps you'd care to hear how it all came about? Lady Cassilis had a hand in it," he quickly added.

At the mention of his stepmother, Alistair surveyed his friend in a sudden new light. "Pray tell what does this concern then?"

"It was during a game of Hunt the Slipper at Lord Brexley's ball," Nicholas replied with a devious twinkle in his eye.

Alistair leveled him a look. The only version of Hunt the Slipper that Nicholas ever played involved copious amounts of wine and women. "You were drunk then," he said bluntly.

"At least, Lady Cassilis thought so." Nicholas chuckled, but then his expression sobered. "She claimied she'd soon find the proof she sought, at last, the 'irrefutable proof'."

The 'irrefutable proof'…his father's dying words.

Alistair crossed to the window and looked out over the snow. Obsessed with building the grandest castle in Scotland, the old earl had bankrupted the Cassilis estate. His solution? Legitimize and make Alistair the heir, thus saving his legacy with his son's self-made fortune. Alistair had always known Lady Cassilis would eventually strike back and contest the will. It had only been a matter of time—even though the courts had assured him the old earl had provided solid proof of his legitimacy and his claim stood unshakable. He'd found his legitimacy astonishing, especially after the manner of his upbringing. It was no small wonder Lady Cassilis did, as well. Yet, irrefutable proof? Now? After almost four years from the day when he'd received a letter from Foster, the Cassilis piper, informing him that his father had requested his immediate presence—at his deathbed.

The mad gallop through the wind driven rain that night had proven fruitless. The old earl hadn't wished to make peace with his estranged, eldest son as Alistair had hoped.

Exhausted and wet to the bone, Alistair had burst into his father's chamber to find him with Lady Cassilis at his side.

Even now, Alistair could feel the heat of his father's gaze as he'd rasped in a labored whisper, "Save the castle."

"The castle?" Alistair had asked.

But the harsh old man had turned to his wife and clutched her arm. "The piper keeps the proof, the irrefutable proof that Alistair is my legitimate heir. The castle. Save the castle."

The shock that rolled over Alistair was dispelled by the venomous look his stepmother directed at him. Her face twisted into a mask of fury that would live forever in his memory.

"You have outwitted me for now, with this false evidence of your mother's marriage," she spat. "But I know better. She was a mere scullery maid. I'll find this *irrefutable proof* and set this travesty to rights."

"Perhaps Lady Cassilis convinced the old piper to finally speak, aye?" Nicholas' deep voice cut through his memories.

Alistair looked at his friend. "Foster knows nothing of the matter."

"You trust the man?"

"I trust Foster with my life," Alistair swore. "Without Angus Foster, I would be nothing."

It was true. Upon his mother's death, as a wee lad, Alistair had been sent to his father. But the earl, having already remarried and fathered another son, saw Alistair as either an embarrassment or—as Alistair suspected—a threat to the purse strings of his new wife's fortune. The earl refused to acknowledge him, and allowed his stepmother to put him to work in the stables. He'd been frightened, lonely, until the piper, Angus Foster, had taken him in as his own. Alistair grew to love the man as a father.

Hard work and Lady Luck favored Alistair. He accumulated a vast fortune and, given his wealth, it was no small wonder that his debt-ridden father had named him heir. Of course, Lady Cassilis hadn't objected then. The earl had squandered every penny she'd possessed. Her only means of support lay in letting Alistair inherit to save the estate—and herself and her son, Charles, along with it.

Alistair gave a bitter laugh. "Lady Cassilis's timing is impeccable. I have only just settled the last of the debts and set the estate to rights. The family coffers are no longer dry."

"Ah, but you have yet to hear the worst." Nicholas rose. "She's once again taken up residence in Culzean."

Alistair retained his share of determination. The windswept lands of his heritage sang in his blood. After spending his life's work saving Culzean, he'd no longer give up the castle without a fight.

He locked gazes with his friend. "How fast can you ride?"

Nicholas' eyes lit. "We ride to roust her from your home?"

"Nae." Alistair shook his head. "I ride to make sure she stays —until I can find out exactly what she's up to and lay this matter to rest, once and for all."

"Even better," Nicholas replied with a grin.

CHAPTER 5

CHARLOTTE RAPPED HER KNUCKLES ON THE BREAKFAST TABLE FOR the third time. "Slower, children." She softened the criticism with a smile. "Forks are to be used, not fingers."

The boy tossed her a dark scowl. Oh, he was a challenge, that one.

"Miss Atchenson," Lord Cassilis's deep voice sounded from the breakfast parlor door. "Might I have a word?"

Charlotte's stomach flipped. A quick look in his direction, hear her the general impression of the man, formidable and aloof in his white linen shirt and a pair of dark gray trousers that hugged muscular thighs. After the embarrassment of hopping through his window the night before, she didn't quite have the courage to look him in the eye. Already, her cheeks heated.

She rose and bobbed a curtsey. Then, in an effort to affect a calm and proper tone, softly replied, "Certainly, my lord."

He stepped into the parlor and motioned toward the far side of the room. She followed until he stopped.

"An important matter has come to my attention, Miss

Atchenson," he said. "I must return to Castle Culzean with haste. I am leaving the children in your care."

"You're leaving?" she blurted.

She looked up into his face. He was clearly distracted and tense, the tendons taut on his neck.

"Yes." He nodded and her gaze caught on his dimpled chin. "My men will escort you and the children safely to Culzean."

She felt only relief at his words—a selfish sort of relief. He made her uncomfortable. They'd known one another only two days and, already, her heart pounded at his every look and her cheeks threatened to burn a dozen shades of red. She shouldn't respond to the man in such a way. After all, she'd just been jilted, hadn't she? Her heart should be a bitter, broken shell. It *certainly* shouldn't be trying to sing every time she carried on the most trivial of conversations with her employer.

"Miss Atchenson?" His gentle inquiry intruded upon her thoughts.

Charlotte started and cursed the heat that crept up her cheeks. Good heavens, had she been staring into the depths of his brilliant green eyes? Licking her suddenly dry lips, she managed to croak, "Yes, my lord?"

To her shock, his gaze dropped to her mouth and noticeably lingered there before returning to her eyes. "I will see you in ten days' time, Miss Atchenson," he said, then turned on his heel and left her staring at his broad shoulders until he stepped out of the room. What was it about the man? His sheer primal intensity sent shivers down her spine.

The scrape of a chair on the wood floor brought her back to the present.

The children. Why couldn't she remember them? She should have had them bid their father goodbye. Of course, the man had left without so much as a grunt in their direction. Had he no heart?

The look of disappointment and anger on her young

charges' faces told her they had noticed as well. Determination shot through her and she rushed to the door and burst into the hallway. Lord Cassilis was halfway down the corridor.

"My lord!" she called.

Lord Cassilis checked his stride and turned.

"Wait there," she ordered. His brow rose in question, but she, whirled and hurried back into the parlor. "Come, children." Charlotte grasped each by the hand and marched them out of the room and down the hall to their father.

As they stopped in front of him, a raven-haired man with startling blue eyes stepped from a room to Lord Cassilis's left. A charming smile pulled at the corner of the man's mouth. The expensive cut of his coat and the quality of his fine leather boots marked him as a noble.

Charlotte directed her attention to Lord Cassilis. "My lord, your children wish to bid you farewell."

The newcomer's brows danced in surprise. "*Alistairrrr?*" he drawled.

"Enough, Nicholas," Lord Cassilis warned before stepping forward with a slight bow. "My apologies, Miss Atchenson. Children," he addressed them in a pleasant rumble, "I fear I find fatherhood rather foreign to me. I meant no disrespect." He looked down at the small, serious faces, then added, "I will see ye in Culzean soon. I bid you farewell."

Charlotte smiled, pleased with his genuine response. The children remained silent. "Children?" She gave their shoulders a nudge.

The young boy rewarded her effort with a sullen scowl.

Charlotte struggled to hold her temper in check. She'd taken his father to task on his behalf, and the young rapscallion chose to repay her with *this* kind of behavior?

Lord Cassilis's deep chuckle echoed in the hall. "Then it is good day, Miss Atchenson." He graced her with a smile dangerous enough to sweep her straight off her feet. "I must be going—as soon as I find my hat."

His hat. Her mind replayed the image of his black, silk hat aflame.

"Good day, my lord," a small voice chimed from her side.

Incredulous, Charlotte glanced down to see the young boy attempting an awkward bow. *The little devil.* So, he didn't want Lord Cassilis knowing about the hat, did he? Had the little troublemaker just handed her the answer to her problem? With the power of blackmail, she could make him dance to *her* tune. Delighted, she curled her lips into a wicked grin. Suddenly aware she'd once again gotten distracted, she glanced up, startled to see both men watching her.

"Then good day," Lord Cassilis said. He turned and said to the man, "Come along, Nicholas."

As both men strode away, Charlotte released a long, silent breath of relief. Two weeks. She had two weeks of freedom to clear her mind. But when her eyes followed Lord Cassilis's thighs as he walked away, she knew she was going to need every hour of those fourteen days to rid her thoughts of the man.

She took a deep breath and shooed the children back to their room and, in short order, had them buttoned in their coats and bundled outside. The crisp morning air did little to clear her thoughts of Lord Cassilis. She hurried the children toward the coach as footmen tied the last trunk to the back of the waiting barouche.

"Hop inside," she said. "We've quite the journey ahead of us."

The boy hesitated. "Oliver," he said with a rush, then added, "And Jane, after me mum."

Jane stilled, not understanding at first, then smothered a delighted smile. Oliver. His name...or was it? The rascal could easily have drummed up the name so as not to be called Abigail. But then, did it matter? At least, she had him talking and, with the threat of the hat, she could get him moving, if need be.

"I must admit, Oliver is more fitting than Abigail," she said, permitting herself a small smile as she waved him toward the barouche. When he didn't move, she paused to prompt, "And?"

He stood, his brows drawn into a scowl. "Why didn't you tell him, Miss?"

Ah, that hat. "Tell him? Tell him what?"

The boy faltered, then leaned closer and answered in a conspiratorial whisper, "The hat. Why didn't you tell him about the hat?"

And relinquish her key to his soul? She placed her cheek close to his and whispered, "What hat? Just this once, I know nothing of a hat."

He drew back with a kind of wary wonder, a grin tugging at his mouth. As if suddenly aware he'd revealed too much, he scowled again and jumped into the carriage, taking his sister with him.

Charlotte followed close behind.

The days passed in a blur. Snow fell, then melted, then fell again.

In daylight, they traveled through wintry wonderlands blanketed in white through the carriage windows. At night, the snow glittered like diamonds in candlelight under the bright light of the moon.

Muddy patches began to show through the snow, until the road turned into a sea of mud. Grime and muck caked the carriage, the children's faces, their shoes and clothes, and even formed a crust on the hem of Charlotte's skirt.

Everywhere Charlotte looked, she saw mud. She felt as if she swam in the stuff. Each night, she dragged the children into yet another inn, pulled off their wet, mud-stained clothes and shoes, and did her best to clean and feed them before settling them to bed. After a day cooped up in the carriage, they were rarely in a mood to obey. Their nightly ritual took far longer than it should. Each evening, she fell into bed exhausted to her very bones, only to awake from a dream of arriving at Castle Culzean, to find she had lost the children along the way.

Oliver's cooperation turned out to be short-lived. By the end of the first day, he'd reverted to sullen behavior, and again refused to participate. With Lord Cassilis gone, she could no longer use the threat of the hat. Jane, however, babbled up a storm. With a never-ending wealth of energy, the child spent the day hopping from seat to seat, peering through the barouche's plate glass windows with wide-eyed wonder and asking endless questions about each tree or clump of dry grass.

Gradually, the rolling hills transformed into wild slopes of harsh, desolate beauty. Dark clouds reappeared on the horizon to mask the sky once again. They rose early and travelled late into the night.

Finally, after what felt like a year, the mutton-chop whiskered footman greeted Charlotte as they stumbled out of the inn and said, "We've been fifteen days on the road, Miss Atchenson. Tonight, you'll sleep in the castle on the edge of the sea."

Charlotte flashed a huge smile of relief, too exhausted to reply.

A hum of excitement underlined the day as they rolled over moorlands dotted with fragile turf huts and through a dense forest of lichen-covered trees. Jane cried in delight at red deer that flicked their ears as they watched the carriage pass. Once the carriage left the forest, it followed a narrow road up the rising coastal cliffs as seagulls swooped overhead, wailing plaintively on a wind that carried the salty tang of the sea.

As they passed an apple orchard late in the day, the horses

picked up speed, as if sensing themselves close to home. Finally, as the sun hovered on the horizon, they rounded the last bend in the road and the castle came into view, a spectacular display of turrets and battlements perched high on the edge of a cliff. Below, the sea pounded a craggy shore pitted with rock pools and patches of sand. She found the place wild, rugged—and as intimidating as the man who presided over it.

The children fell silent, she along with them, their eagerness to arrive replaced with a general unease that the long, tedious weeks now seemed to be ending too fast.

Before she could bolster her courage, the carriage rolled down the drive. Trees lined both sides of the road. Then the carriage rolled under a ruined archway and past a cluster of outbuildings presided over by a fine clock tower. At last, it reached the castle proper.

"Whoa there, lads," the coachman called to the bays, and brought them to a stop before the castle's massive main doors.

The footmen dismounted and the mutton-chop whiskered footman opened the carriage door. Charlotte sat still, too aware of her suddenly flailing courage, as well as the children's stares. She had to be confident. Strong. She smiled gently, then scooted to the door and allowed the footman to hand her out.

The wind tore through the open courtyard and nearly ripped her bonnet from her head. Charlotte clapped a hand on the hat, turned her head aside, and grabbed her skirts with her free hand lest her legs be bared in seconds.

As the children exited the carriage behind her, the main door opened and an elderly, crag-faced man dressed in dark trousers and clutching a green Cassilis plaid cloak about his bowed shoulders hurried toward the carriage. A redheaded, ample-bosomed, white-aproned maid followed him.

They reached the coach as the children huddled beside Charlotte.

"Welcome, welcome, I'm Angus Foster, the Cassilis piper,

but call me Foster, lass," the elderly man introduced himself with an openhearted smile. "You must be Miss Atchenson, the governess."

"Charlotte." She raised her voice above the buffeting winds. "Charlotte Atchenson, but please call me Charlotte."

Foster's wrinkled cheeks split into a grin and his gaze fell upon the children. Turning to the young freckle-faced maid behind him, he added, "This is Meg. She will care for the bairns now."

The words struck Charlotte to the core. Care for the bairns? She frowned.

"'Tis my task now, Miss Atchenson," Meg said in a loud, booming voice. She waved the children toward the castle. "Come with me now, ye wee folk. I've warm tea and biscuits in the nursery, and fresh, clean, new clothes for the both of you. Losh, but you look asleep on your feet."

Charlotte watched them go, suddenly on the verge of tears. Had she been replaced? Why? Had Lord Cassilis changed his mind? Had Lady Prescott or some other personage convinced him that hiring her was a mistake, after all? Heavens…had he discovered her mastery of the French language included only the colorful words one would never repeat in polite society?

She turned to the piper in dismay. "I fail to understand." A strong gust of wind tore through the courtyard, ripping the words from her lips.

The piper crooked a finger and beckoned her to follow, then hurried to the castle. She entered behind him, the wind nearly pushing her through the open door.

Once inside, the old man faced her. "Och, the winds blow bitter today, lass, don't they now?"

Charlotte struggled to blink back tears. What was she to do in Scotland? Alone. Homeless.

"If you will follow me." The old piper was already shuffling away. "His lordship has requested your immediate presence in the library."

Immediate presence. Charlotte's heart sank to her toes. She followed the piper through the dimly lit entrance hall and past a massive display of swords and pistols mounted on the wall. Beyond the weapons display, a grand, central, oval staircase swept upward. She paused on the first rich, red-carpeted step behind him and looked up the twisting stairs to the magnificent, white Corinthian columns ringing the floors above and to the domed glass cupola at the very top.

The piper glanced back at her. "Come, lass," he gently encouraged. "His lordship awaits."

Charlotte nodded woodenly and forced her feet to carry her up the stairs.

The piper led her to the second floor and down a passage to the left. They passed under crystal chandeliers ablaze with white candles and strode past portraits in gilded frames. Here and there, a marble-topped table stood elegantly off to the side, holding ornate brass, lit tiered candlesticks that provided glimpses of more elegant rooms and passageways. The castle looked like paradise—especially after more than a week of traveling through mud.

Finally, the piper stopped in front of an old, massive oak door. He knocked, then opened the door, and nodded for her to enter. Charlotte stepped into a large room lit by a crackling fire contained by a grate of iron pelicans. The orange glow penetrated enough shadows to discern shelves filled with books, with tapestries hung between the shelves. The comforting smell of leather hung in the air.

Hesitantly, she approached the hearth and two wing-backed chairs upholstered in gold-striped velvet. On a small table positioned between the chairs sat a chessboard, several empty glasses, and a crystal flask filled with a light amber liquid.

"Thank you, Foster," Lord Cassilis's deep voice broke the silence.

Charlotte jerked as the piper bowed and left, closing the large door behind him.

The next moment, Lord Cassilis stepped into view from the shadows near the shelves halfway between the door and the hearth. He wore a loose, white, puff-sleeved shirt with his cravat undone and his brocade vest unbuttoned. Her mouth dropped open, the intimacy of his undress heating the tips of her ears.

"Miss Atchenson." A smile creased his cheeks. "Please, join me by the fire."

Charlotte took a deep breath. "My lord." She dipped into a curtsey. "I—"

"Have a seat, please." He motioned toward the two chairs as he strode toward them. "You have only just arrived. I dare say, you must be dead on your feet."

He waited until she took a seat, then lowered himself in the opposite chair. As he leaned back and stretched out his long legs, she couldn't help but notice how his breeches showcased his muscular thighs, nor did she miss the tanned flesh revealed by his open collar. Memories of her hands on his bare chest at the inn popped into her head.

Steady on there, Charlotte, she warned. *Steady on.* She had her employment to fret over now, not the firmness of the man's chest.

Lord Cassilis snagged the crystal flask from the table. "I know you are quite weary, Miss Atchenson, so I shall not take much of your time."

Charlotte swallowed and nodded.

"Highland whisky," he announced.

He filled two glasses, then handed her one. Charlotte accepted it. Why was he circling around the issue? Why couldn't he tell her outright just why he'd replaced her?

He watched her. "Take a drink, Miss Atchenson," he suggested. "You look as if you could use it."

She looked down at the liquid in her glass. She'd never tasted whisky. Her father and Captain Edwards had insisted she abstain from alcohol. But now? She certainly felt in need of bolstering. She took a sip. The whisky dug a hot furrow down her throat.

She coughed and dragged in a harsh breath. "It tastes like perfume," she wheezed.

Lord Cassilis chuckled.

Charlotte cleared her throat and looked up at him. "My lord," she croaked. "Meg…" Tears burned her eyes. She struggled to gather her frazzled nerves.

"Meg?" he echoed, at first sounding bewildered. "Ah yes, Meg. I've assigned her to the children's care."

She couldn't deny it. There it was. He *had* ended her employment. The stress from the past few weeks crashed down around her. Tears welled in her eyes. In an effort to mask them, she brought her glass to her lips and tossed the whisky back all at once. She braced herself for the fiery path of the liquid down her throat, and managed to only gag. The whisky reached her belly and a pleasantly warm sensation fluttered there.

"Easy, lass," Lord Cassilis cautioned.

She mustered her courage and met his gaze. "Might I ask why, my lord?"

"Why?" He frowned.

"We've only just arrived, my lord." A strange lightheadedness made her feel disconnected from her thoughts. "We traveled two long weeks. Surely, surely…" *Please, she begged him silently, please let me stay.* "Tell me what I must do and I will do it, my lord."

He tilted his head. "I have heard plenty from the footman. More than enough to settle that score."

She squinted at him. The footman? Which one? They'd all

seemed so kind. She'd never thought a one of them to be the sort who would knife her in the back. She glanced at her glass.

"Allow me." He refilled her glass.

Charlotte swiped at tears with the back of her hand, then drained her glass again.

Lord Cassilis snatched the glass from her. "That's highland whisky, lass, not water." He laughed outright. "From the looks of it, you've had enough." Setting her empty glass on the table, he crossed his legs. "I admit, I am confused as to what you mean."

She frowned, decidedly dizzy, but suddenly found it much easier to talk. "Why are you ending my employment, my lord? I have only just arrived. Is it...is it my father?"

His brows rose. "Ending your employment? Pray tell, where did ye hear such a thing?"

A flicker of hope surged inside her. "But, Mary," she said, then paused. The name sounded off. It was. "Ah, yes, Meg. But Meg?"

His face lit with sudden understanding—along with a healthy dose of amusement. "I assigned Meg as the children's *nursemaid*. You, my dear, are the governess. Manage them all as you please. As governess, you are responsible for their upbringing. I could hardly expect you to take care of them both, entirely by yourself."

"Then you're not letting me go?" she whispered. But the footman...hadn't he said something about the footman? She concentrated in an effort to pierce the haze surrounding her thoughts. Finally, she managed to form the words, "The footman?"

"He only sings your praises, Miss Atchenson. I have received letters of your progress along the way." Lord Cassilis chuckled again. "In fact, if he were not a happily married man, I would think he would have fallen in love with you."

Relief washed over her. A giddy sensation filled her with

warmth. "In love with me?" A small giggle escaped her lips. She clamped a hand over her mouth.

Charlotte stared into his gorgeous emerald green eyes. He was handsome. Too handsome. She'd hoped the journey would clear her mind of such thoughts, but it hadn't. One look at his chiseled cheekbones, angular nose, and dimpled chin—a formidably masculine dimpled chin—and she was lost once again. Her stomach fluttered.

She hiccupped. "Damnation," she mumbled, then realized she'd just hiccupped *and* cursed. She cleared her throat. "I beg your pardon, Lord Cassslsi..." She paused. Something about the name sounded wrong. Charlotte frowned and tried again. "Lord Cassilis." Whe tried her best to enunciate each syllable.

"You're drunk, lass." His sensual lips curved up at the corners.

She forgot what she was trying to say. It was too hard to concentrate around the man. He was simply too handsome. What would he do if she ran her finger down his hard-cut jaw and over the bottom lip of his expressive mouth? Small wonder the poor laundress had fallen prey to his charms. What woman wouldn't?

"You're simply too...handsome." She yawned. "It's rather unfair."

She blinked twice and frowned again. Had she just said that aloud?

CHAPTER 6

ALISTAIR VALIANTLY STRUGGLED TO SUPPRESS HIS AMUSEMENT AS he watched Charlotte succumbed to the whisky's spell. A twinge of guilt stabbed, but only a twinge. He'd underestimated just how much—or little—she could imbibe before succumbing to the powerful drink. He should've known her delicate constitution would fail to withstand the second glass, but then, he hadn't expected her to down it all in one go like the town drunk.

She frowned, leaned sideways in her chair and squinted. "You're simply too…handsome. It's rather unfair."

Alistair tensed. What had she said? By God, the woman thought him too handsome? His heart began to pound. She found him attractive?

She nibbled her bottom lip. His blood burned. How he wanted that mouth. Such a delectable mouth with such pink lips, plump and full, begging to be kissed. As ever, several rebellious curls had escaped her bun, dragging his gaze to the sensual line of her neck. A coil of desire wound through his body.

"Did I say that aloud, Lord Cssils…" She seemed to wrestle with each word.

He shouldn't have poured the second whisky, but he had to admit he felt sorely pressed to regret it. "That I was handsome? Aye, lass, you did."

Her pupils widened in the firelight as her lips formed a perfect circle. "Oooh," she whispered, then added in a rush, "Lord Casssilllis…may I call you Alistair, instead? It is so much easier to say."

Alistair chuckled. "Only if I may call you Charlotte."

Charlotte nodded, her hazel eyes sparkling. "Please do." She wrinkled her nose. "Forgive me. I shouldn't have said…"

"There's nothing to forgive," he assured. "If anything, it is I who should beg forgiveness for pouring the second whisky, lass."

"It tastes dreadful." She waved her fingers. "But it warms the toes."

The toes? He sipped his whisky, then replied, "Indeed."

She hiccupped, then covered her mouth again with her hands. "I thought you no longer needed my services," she confessed in a whisper. "I thought you were letting me go."

"Quite the contrary," he replied.

The smile spreading over her lovely face beguiled him. Let her go? She'd fascinated him from the moment he laid eyes upon her in Lady Prescott's drawing room. He'd thought it a fleeting fascination. In the past two weeks, he'd convinced himself he felt nothing extraordinary toward her, nothing beyond the interest a man *should* feel toward the governess of his own niece and nephew. He'd been wrong. His reaction to her was much stronger this time.

She yawned and relaxed against the chair back. "Then that is well," she murmured. "I have no desire to sleep on the streets."

The words caught his interest. "Surely, you have relatives somewhere, Charlotte?"

"The devil I do," she retorted in a very unladylike manner. "Hardhearted and uncaring wretches, the lot of them—and the Captain, as well."

"Captain?" he repeated.

Charlotte grimaced in distaste. "My fian…fian…" she struggled to enunciate.

He tensed. "Fiancé?"

She pointed a finger at him with a lopsided grin. "*That's* the word."

It wasn't a word he liked.

She cocked her head. "He said I shouldn't look at that crimson dress. I was just looking. Just looking. He said a decent woman wouldn't even do that. Look. But it was beautiful. A dream."

The man sounded like an ass. Alistair took another sip from his glass. "Where is this captain now?"

Charlotte lifted her chin. "Let's not speak of him."

"Very well, then," he granted with a nod. It didn't matter. He'd have Foster find out. And if her fiancé dared show his face at Culzean, Alistair would have a choice word or two to say on Charlotte's behalf.

A silence fell between them and he thought she'd fallen asleep, but she suddenly sat up and clucked her tongue against her teeth. "They even took my mother's cookery book," she said with heat.

"They?" Alistair queried softly.

"The creditors." Her tongue tripped over the word. "It was the only thing I had left of her." She scowled and passed her hand over her head, as if it hurt.

"This captain of yours let them take it?" Alistair asked.

"He gave me ten shillings," she replied in a bitter tone. "Ten."

"A beggar's pittance. I find myself unimpressed with the man."

She closed her eyes.

Again, he thought she'd fallen asleep, but she roused herself yet again. "Now, you," she slurred her words. "You may look quite intimitia…intimidd…in…"

"Intimidating?" he supplied.

"Yes, that." She nodded emphatically. "But under it all… you're the honorable…sort, aren't you now…?"

"Honorable? I daresay, there are others who might disagree." His stepmother came to mind.

She hiccupped then relaxed against the chair. This time, her lush, dark lashes fell over her eyes and her full lips relaxed. He watched her slump sideways in the chair. How could her fiancé let her fall into such dire circumstances and offer a mere ten shillings of relief? What did she see in such a wretch? Yet… she was engaged. If he were the honorable sort—as she thought him—he would do the honorable thing and walk away.

He pushed from his chair, crossed to the window and stared out into the night. He considered the issue from different angles, but after a good hour, he still reached the same conclusion. He didn't *want* to walk away. He didn't think he could. The lass hadn't married the ass, yet. Perhaps he could make her see she deserved a worthier man. And if the captain returned from wherever he'd gone and found his fiancée in love with someone else…then so be it.

"May the better man win," he murmured.

At the sound of retching, he whirled in time to see Charlotte kneeling over the fire. He hurried to her side. She moaned as he arrived, and she gagged again.

"Forgive me, lass," he murmured, this time regretting the second glass of whisky. "Let's get you to your room." He grasped her arm and pulled her to her feet.

She swayed unsteadily. Alistair slid an arm around her waist and she clung to him and laid her head on his chest.

"Charlotte." Her name sounded intimate on his lips. "Come, I'll help you upstairs."

She answered with a soft snore.

He could've called someone to escort her. But didn't. Instead, he looped his arm under her knees and lifted her against his chest. She was light and delicate in his arms. As he strode toward the door, she moaned a little before nestling her head against his shoulder. Alistair paused at the door and stared down at her, more than a little attracted and somewhat amused she'd likely remember nothing of the encounter.

He pushed the door open with his foot. Low-burning candles in the hallway, shone tiny islands of light to guide his walk down the hallway. He reached the stairs leading up to the nursery and had a foot on the first stair when a woman stepped from behind a Corinthian column to his right. He started and swore under his breath. So, his stepmother had finally arrived. Being waylaid by her like this was what he got for leaving instructions that he wasn't to be disturbed during his meeting with Charlotte.

"Lady Cassilis," he said through gritted teeth.

She stood, a dark, shadowy form on the edge of the grand oval stair. The flickering candlelight cast her in an almost ghoulish glow. Her narrow face and upturned nose looked like a caricature and her gray-streaked brown hair made her look ten years older than her fifty-five years. She glared, her furrowed brows set in a disgruntled, judgmental frown, and her mouth tugged down in permanent disapproval. That was no surprise. He'd never seen her smile.

Her stare shifted to Charlotte. "Who is that?"

He quashed the impulse to ignore her and answered with a cool, "This is Charlotte Atchenson. The governess."

"The governess?" she repeated waspishly. "The woman Lady

Prescott mentioned in her letter? Heavens, Alistair, you brought her *here*?" Her lips pressed into a thin line of hatred.

So, the two old biddies had been talking. He simply wasn't in the mood. "What brings you to Castle Culzean?" Would she gloat? Admit the truth? Or would she lie? He could never fathom how her vile mind worked.

"I've come to stay, until it pleases me to do otherwise." Her thin nostrils flared and he half wondered if she might charge him. "It is my right."

Technically, she no longer possessed such rights but, despite his better judgement, he couldn't cast his own stepmother out on the streets—no matter how odious and vile she was.

"I can't imagine you relish the thought of living here with me." He adjusted Charlotte as she snored in his arms.

"Perhaps it is *you* who will leave, Alistair." A gleam of hope lit her eyes.

Ah, her irrefutable proof. "Foster knows nothing of what you seek," he said bluntly. "You're clutching at straws, madam. The deed is done. Truth is, the courts have declared the matter over and we're likely never to find this proof that would settle the question of when, where and even if the earl wed my mother."

She stepped back, clearly shocked at his directness. With the many hateful words she'd spewed and deeds she'd done to harm him over the years, he failed to see why she would bother with such charades.

"The courts declared the matter done," he repeated. "We must move forward, Lady Cassilis, and find a way to tolerate each other. Now, if you'll excuse me." He turned and started up the stairs.

"I will find my proof, Alistair," his stepmother hissed at his back. "Irrefutable proof. Your day is coming."

He paused and looked at her over his shoulder. "Until then, Lady Cassilis. Good evening."

He left her, standing in silent outrage, and quickly climbed to the nursery, a pleasant suite of rooms overlooking the sea. A light flickered under the door, and he entered to find Meg rocking the wee lassie by the fire, the lad asleep on a plaid nearby.

"Sit, please." He stayed her with a smile as she started to rise.

"Losh, my lord," the freckle-faced Meg exclaimed, her kindly eyes dropping on Charlotte. "What happened?"

Alistair glanced down at Charlotte, still nestled against his shoulder. "My fault," he admitted wryly. "I gave her more highland whisky than she had the stomach for."

Meg snorted a laugh.

"Her room?" Alistair lifted a brow at the three doors on the opposite wall.

She pointed to the middle one. Alistair nodded thanks, then crossed to the room. He opened the door with his shoulder and continued to the small bed where he laid her down. As she curled on her side, he picked up the folded blanket at the foot of the bed and covered her. A sense of contentment washed over him as he returned to the sitting room once again.

"Bless you, sir, for your big heart," Meg said.

He paused and waited.

"The wee lad and lassie." The maid darted a look at the boy as she ran her fingers over the little girl's red curls. "You've a rare kindness in you, sir."

"Let's keep that a secret, shall we?" he teased with a sardonic twist of his lip.

"Aye," she laughed.

He bid her goodnight and left the nursery. Minutes later, he entered the library once again to find Nicholas in his chair with his booted feet propped on the table.

"She's here," his friend said. "Lady Cassilis."

Alistair seated himself in the chair opposite him. "I just spoke with her. I have heard nothing new, but I'll have her watched, all the same. No doubt, when your guests arrive, she'll use the distractions to carry out whatever nefarious plan she's concocted."

"To be sure," Nicholas agreed with a bored yawn.

Alistair regarded him. "Is not your own true love to arrive on the morrow? You seem afflicted with a melancholy languor or a decided lack of interest. Surely, your ardor has no' cooled already?"

The raven-haired baronet shot him a ruffled look, then picked up Alistair's unfinished glass of whisky from the table and drained its contents. He set the glass back down. "I confess, her face has already faded from memory. Can a man truly recall a woman after a separation of a day or two?"

Alistair snorted. Not once in the past two weeks had he forgotten the spark of Charlotte's eyes, but he wasn't inclined to offer the observation. "I fear I cannot say," he replied.

"Cannot…or will not?" Nicholas murmured. With a sigh, he rose. "I bid you goodnight."

Alistair watched his friend leave, then sat in his chair and turned his gaze to the dying fire.

ALISTAIR ENTERED THE BREAKFAST PARLOR IN A STARTLING GOOD mood. Yes, Lady Cassilis and all her intrigue had arrived with the full intent to cause him harm, but he scarcely spared her a thought. Why should he? After all, there was so much to enjoy in the day. He glanced out the window at the driving sheets of rain that battered the glass. He shrugged. A good mood did not require the sun.

A maid hurried in and set his plate of eggs and Westmoreland ham on the table, alongside a stack of the week's papers delivered by the post. Alistair seated himself and picked up *The*

Morning Chronicle. Setting aside the gossip section, he proceeded to scan the paper.

"My dear fellow." Nicholas' deep laugh sounded from the door. "Leaving the gossip column untouched? You are missing the best part."

Alistair peered at him over the paper. "Dare I read a newspaper for news?"

Nicholas entered, the corners of his ice-blue eyes crinkling with humor, a humor that vanished the moment he sat down.

Alistair sighed. "What ails you, now?"

"I'll say it and have done. When will you do me the honor of an introduction to Miss Atchenson?"

Alistair slammed the paper down on the table. "Never." The word erupted from his lips. "Is not Catherine Brexley enough for you?"

"I fail—" Nicholas began when shattering glass sounded in the hallway.

Both men jumped to their feet and dashed through the door in time to witness Charlotte flying down the grand oval staircase toward them, her dark curls bouncing over her shoulders and her pink mouth set in a determined line.

Alistair started toward her. His nephew shot from the stairs and tried to veer around him. Alistair seized the boy's collar. "What mischief have you fostered this fine morning, young rascal?" he asked the boy wriggling in his grasp.

The child winced.

Alistair took in his crumpled white shirtsleeves, wrinkled trousers, and uncombed hair, and said in mock sternness, "You look quite the ragamuffin."

"Pardon me, my lord," Charlotte arrived breathless.

Alistair's heart leapt. Would her cheeks flush like that while she lay beneath him? He couldn't halt a flick of his gaze to the swell of her breasts as they rose and fell. Her simple blue dress molded to her slender figure almost indecently. Zounds, she was beautiful. And her lips? He was becoming obsessed with them. He'd never seen a softer, sweeter, or more tempting pair in his life.

"A wild hellion," a poisonous voice ripped through his distracted muse.

His lust vanished. Alistair shifted his gaze to Lady Cassilis. She descended the stairs, dressed in a fine peach taffeta gown, a look of withering reproach on her face.

"A miserable boy," she said as she reached the final steps. She sidestepped something and Alistair caught sight of shards of a china basin on the hallway floor—the source of the crash.

Lady Cassilis reached them and turned toward Charlotte. "A governess is to instill the social graces above all else, etiquette, *manners*—do you understand the meaning of those words?"

The boy wriggled in Alistair's grasp in a clearly attempt to flee this new adversary. Alistair couldn't blame him. With a firm grip on the lad's collar, he addressed his stepmother, "I suggest you practice what you preach, Lady Cassilis." She drew a sharp breath, but he cut off any retort, "If you cannot be civil, then say nothing at all, lest you wear out your welcome."

Her head snapped in his direction, then her eyes dropped to the boy and her expression softened. Alistair remained still. Had her maternal instincts stirred, at long last? The boy was, after all, her grandchild. Then, the cold anger Alistair had grown accustomed to clouded her face once again.

"Your brat, to be sure." Her thin jowls jiggled with repressed anger.

Alistair stared in shock. Charles had acknowledged the children when he abandoned them on Lady Prescott's door. Lady Cassilis knew right *well* they were her very own grandchildren, sired by her son.

Anger flashed through him. "The hardness of your heart has always astounded me, Lady Cassilis. Until now, I thought you had at least some sense. However, it appears old age has fossilized your heart. Have a care. Where it comes to these children, I shall not tolerate your venom."

With a huff, she gathered her skirts and swept from the hallway.

Alistair turned his attention to the boy. "What have you to say for yourself, lad?"

The boy widened his nostrils, defiant, but remained silent.

"Oliver?" Charlotte prompted.

Oliver. So, she'd ferreted out the lad's name? Of course, she had. Alistair looked down at the young boy. "The basin on the floor, Oliver. Your doing, I assume?"

The boy's green eyes flashed.

Alistair blinked, suddenly struck by the lad's likeness to his father. Well, the resemblance would end there. He wouldn't allow the boy to follow Charles' ne'er-do-well footsteps.

"It is time you learn the value of a shilling," Alistair said.

Oliver's eyes widened. "You brought me here to work?"

Alistair cursed silently. He was bungling this whole affair. The last thing he intended was for the boy to feel the pain of being sent off to work. "Every man should know the worth of a good day's labor," he said gently. "There's no shame in that."

"He meant no harm, my lord," Charlotte said. "He is just a boy."

Alistair nodded. "Aye. Come along, Oliver."

He released the lad's collar, but grasped his forearm and led him down the hall with Charlotte trotting alongside. She cast him a worried glance as they continued south and entered the Blue Drawing Room, the wonder of Castle Culzean.

Light blue silk covered walls trimmed with delicate plasterwork of flower vases and gryphons. A plush red carpet spanned the floor, and in the center of the blue-painted ceiling, the architect had embedded a round oil painting. A dozen portraits adorned the walls, but it was to a portrait hung over the hearth that Alistair headed.

"Now, here's a man who didn't understand the value of a shilling." He gave a dry chuckle. "Your grandfather. The very devil himself, and a more arrogant, harsher man never lived. He left this estate in financial ruin."

Oliver glanced up at him, small brows furrowed in surprise. Alistair guided him to the next painting. "This is his father, a man who let the fine heritage of his clan crumble away while he wasted his life in cardrooms and other unsavory places."

Oliver's brows knotted tighter.

"There are others." Alistair waved his hand to encompass other portraits. "Some more honorable than their foolish descendants who bled the land dry. This is your heritage. They are the ones who made your clan what it is and established a fortress here." He paused to look at the first two paintings once again, then released the lad and extended his hands toward him. "These are the hands of a working man, Oliver. A man who started life just like you, the son of a maid servant and one of the men above the fireplace. There is nothing wrong with being a working man. A working man saved this crumbling estate, never forget that."

The lad looked up to him and, for once, he didn't appear angry.

"Follow me." Alistair turned on his heel and headed toward the library.

He didn't glance back to see if the lad followed. The swish of Charlotte's dress assured him that she accompanied him. When he arrived at the library, he was pleased to find Oliver behind him.

Alistair strode to the shelf near the window and ran his fingers over the spines of the fine leather volumes until he found the one he sought, a beginner's Latin grammar. Selecting the book, he turned and looked down at the boy.

"You've your whole life before you, Oliver. I will see you make something of yourself. You're a Cassilis and I'll see you uphold the dignity of the clan."

The boy frowned.

Alistair pushed the book against the boy's chest. "As recompense for the china basin, you are to copy the first chapter. Neatly. I expect it before supper. Now, you may go."

Oliver stared, his mouth working, but he turned and stiffly walked toward the door.

Alistair smiled.

As Charlotte started to follow the lad, he called, "A word, Miss Atchenson."

She froze a moment, then faced him and dropped a curtsey.

"Nae." He raised a hand, palm out. "Please, I grow weary of the formality."

She straightened in surprise. "Aye, my lord."

"My lord? Did you not say you wished to call me Alistair?" he teased.

Her brow furrowed in confusion, then horror widened her hazel eyes. So, she *did* remember.

With her color heightening, she lifted her chin a notch. "Last night…was much like a dream—"

"A dream? So, I appear in your dreams?" He injected a touch of suggestion into his tone.

She blinked and her lips parted again, but before she could reply, a sharp knock sounded on the door.

Alistair turned as Lady Cassilis entered. Charlotte bolted toward the door. He couldn't blame her. She paused before Lady Cassilis and curtseyed, allowing him to catch an unexpected and delightful glimpse of her trim ankle, then she fled.

"Really, Alistair, your manners lack breeding." Lady Cassilis marched into the room.

Breeding. Her favorite word. The woman obsessed over the proper placement of people in society. He released a sigh.

"Should you not be out searching for this proof you seek? There's no piper here in the library."

She blinked, appearing somewhat taken aback, but switched subjects. "Dare you foist off your own bastards as my son's children? What nerve you have. Those children have nothing to do with *me*. I will *not* allow you to stain my son's good name."

He pinned her with a stare. She would never cease to shock him. "They are your grandchildren, Lady Cassilis, Charles' children. Until you can behave in a civil manner, keep away from them. Might I suggest London or even Paris?"

She clucked her tongue. "So ill-behaved, so uneducated. Small wonder that Lady Prescott's alarmed. And that hussy you call a governess? She dresses like a beggar. Why, such a shameful—"

"Silence!" he thundered.

Her chin trembled. "Dare you insult me in my own house?" She curled her fingers into fists.

"Castle Culzean is no longer your house," he replied sharply. "It is mine."

"For now, Alistair." Her face flushed a dark red. "For now."

He watched her leave, and feared he had just goaded a deadly snake.

CHAPTER 7

CHARLOTTE GROANED, WANTING TO MELT RIGHT THROUGH THE floor. She'd hoped it was just a dream. But after seeing the amusement in those emerald eyes, she knew it hadn't been a dream at all. She had, indeed, asked Lord Cassilis if she could call him by name and she'd told him he was handsome. She quickened her pace toward the nursery, her cheeks burning. She would never drink highland whisky again. She would have to hide from him, at least a month or more—maybe forever. Devil take it, and more besides. What had come over her?

What of the way he'd looked at her in the library? Her breath caught at the recollection of that ravenously sensual expression. If he ever unleashed the full force of that charm, she would fall in the blink of an eye. Her heart thudded. Heavens, why did such a possibility excite her? Where was her shame?

Shaking off her thoughts, she opened the nursery door. Meg's rocking chair stood empty before the fire, but she could hear the muffled sounds of her voice, along with Jane's giggles, coming from behind the little girl's bedroom door. Oliver was nowhere to be seen. She hurried to his bedroom door, paused, then peered through the crack. The boy stood by the window, hugging the Latin grammar to his thin chest. He looked so lost, so sad, that the reprimand died on her lips.

Charlotte eased the door open. "Oliver?"

He jerked and his eyes shuttered at once. Jutting out his chin, he met her gaze and the all-too-familiar stubbornness ran rampant over his face.

So, he still wanted to hide his pain behind anger. She pointed over her shoulder at the table in the nursery. "You've a chapter to copy, do you not, young master? You'd best hurry."

"I don't know any letters," he half snarled, even as he clutched the book tighter.

"I didn't think you did," she replied in a matter-of-fact way. She clapped her hands and pointed to the table again. "But that doesn't stop you from making your best effort. I will find quill and paper, and you will spend the day copy what you can. You must show something to your father before supper, do you not agree?"

He hesitated, then nodded. Once.

Charlotte turned away, unable to halt a grin. So, the little devil wanted to impress his father. It was a great start. If she managed to make him sit for an hour and scratch out three letters, she would consider the day a success.

He emerged from the bedroom and went to the table as she rummaged in the nearby cupboard for writing supplies. The first shelf revealed several books, including one titled *The Fine Art of Deportment*. She flipped through the pages, then set it aside to read later. In short order, she located a small glass bottle of ink, a quill, and several sheets of paper. After Charlotte set the boy to work, she stepped back to dust her hands. A sudden sharp knock on the door startled them both.

"Eyes down, Oliver," she ordered, then answered the door.

A young maid with reddish-brown curls peeked out from under her mob-cap fidgeted on the threshold. "Lady Cassilis wishes to see you, Miss." She winced with a commiserating smile. "I am to take you there, at once."

A shiver of dread danced down Charlotte's spine. Clearing her throat, she replied, "Let me tell Meg."

The maid nodded, then whispered, "Best hurry, Miss. Lady Cassilis's not one to cross."

From the little she'd seen of the woman, Charlotte agreed. She quickly informed Meg, then followed the maid through the castle, up and down stairs and across floors until she'd lost her sense of direction. All too soon, they entered Lady Cassilis's room.

The room was large and finely furnished with a magnificent pink floral carpet, plush armchairs, and an elegantly inlaid Baroque-styled secretary desk. Sweeping, gold-velvet curtains covered the windows. Lady Cassilis's sour expression appeared at odds with the cheerful fire before which she sat.

"My lady." Charlotte curtsied.

The woman subjected her to a drawn-out inspection. Finally, she snapped her fan open and spoke. "It seems you must be taught your proper place in this house. You are a domestic, a servant, and nothing more. As such, you cannot indulge in unsuitable familiarity with your employer. Lord Cassilis is a man of rank. On my *word*, I've never seen such scandalous behavior in a governess. *Never*, in all my *days*."

Charlotte's heart began to pound. "Please, my lady, how have I offended?" She struggled to speak through suddenly numb lips.

"The impudence," Lady Cassilis pressed on. "Do you think Lord Cassilis to be your personal footman? To carry you to your bed whenever you're drunk out of your wits?"

Charlotte froze. He'd carried her to her bed? She had no recollection of that. She barely recalled snippets of their conversation in the library before awakening in her bed with a raging headache.

"Do you understand the importance of a room such as the Blue Drawing Room?" Lady Cassilis rapped her fan on the arm of her chair to capture Charlotte's attention.

Charlotte jerked. The Blue Drawing Room? Alistair had taken Oliver there to show him his roots and the value of hard work, but she knew Lady Cassilis meant nothing of the sort. Quickly, she shook her head.

"It is a measure of society," the woman said. "It is the line. It separates those who are born to sit in it and those who are born to clean it. Are you confused as to which side of that line you stand?"

Her remarks stung like a slap on the face. Charlotte swallowed. "Nae, my lady."

"Then I will see you act in accordance with your rank." Rising to her feet, she huffed. "We have guests arriving this very moment. I expect you to stand with the other domestics to greet them. Make yourself presentable and go at once."

Charlotte fled.

The sympathetic mob-capped maid caught her arm at the door. "Quickly, Miss." She dragged Charlotte to a nearby mirror. "They've already started the line downstairs. Here, I'll help."

Flustered, Charlotte squinted at her reflection. Her cheeks stood out as two bright pink spots under her wide hazel eyes. She looked terrified. Perhaps, because she was. The maid tucked her unruly stray curls into her bun in the back, she worked on the front. Her gown, though serviceable, had begun to look a little frayed and worn. She'd do well to find another dress or two, before Lady Cassilis complained over the state of her clothes. Biting her lip, Charlotte focused on her hair, but when a curl she'd already tucked into place for the third time sprang out again, she dropped her hands and blew the remaining hair out of her eyes with an exasperated huff.

"It's impossible," she said with a rueful smile to the young woman still vainly trying to tame her curls. "My hair goes whither it will. If it displeases her ladyship, then I will go whither the wind blows. I can change, but I fear, my hair cannot."

The maid laughed shyly. "Aye, it is good enough, and with the wildness of the winds outside, we'll all suffer the same fate. Who's to notice only yours?"

Lady Cassilis, Charlotte thought pointedly, but she knew better than to say such things aloud. The woman had the eyes of a hawk, and no doubt, the ears of an owl.

They hurried down the servants' stairs to the foyer. When they neared the door, Charlotte slowed while Meg continued outside to the tail-end of the servants' line that stretched from the castle entrance to the drive. Charlotte couldn't take her eyes off Alistair, who waited with his friend Nicholas at the driveway to greet the approaching carriage. Her heart began to thud. Wind whipped a light mist. His hair tossed against his forehead. He looked so tall and handsome in his tight gray trousers, Hessian boots, and dark blue cutaway coat with its brass buttons, long tails, and standup collar.

Charlotte halted at the door. She didn't want to face him. She glanced around, tempted to duck away and hide, but Lady Cassilis chose that moment to sweep down the grand staircase. Charlotte hurried out the door. Gusts of wind tugged her hair. In seconds, the primping of the moments before was undone. She winced, wondering how long they would have to wait.

From the corner of her eye, Charlotte glimpsed Lady Cassilis emerge from the castle. Despite the wind and rain, she paused to inspect the servants as she pulled on her long, white gloves. Their eyes met. Charlotte quickly glanced away and swallowed. There was no running now. The jingle of harnesses and the crunch of wheels on gravel announced the final arrival of the carriage as the coachman pulled rein and Alistair and Nicholas stepped forward to open the door. Charlotte spied a small, delicate shoe and the hem of a fine pink gown before something flashed in the corner of her eye. Startled, she glanced up. Her heart leapt into her throat.

Oliver.

Wearing a bright green hat with a red feather, the boy dashed to the side of the drive and along the low, stone wall, headed toward the clock tower.

Her heart sank. Whispering a hasty "Excuse me" to the servants flanking either side, Charlotte hurried down the steps, then took off at a dead run after him. She followed the stone wall, calling his name. But the fierce winds ripped the words from her mouth, and he was far too quick on his feet. She clapped a hand to her cap. Before she'd closed the distance half way, he darted under the clock tower and disappeared from sight.

Charlotte burst into the clock tower courtyard right after him, only to find it empty. Turning in a circle, she gasped between breaths, "Oliver! Come here, at once!"

There was no response.

At the sudden whinny of a horse, she darted through the back archway and down a short drive leading to a long, low stone building perched near the edge of the cliff and protected from the sea below by a stone wall. The smell of horse and a mound of hay near the open door, told her she'd reached the stables. Charlotte yanked up her skirts, ran to the door and darted inside. At once, she spied Oliver's green hat poking above a nearby stall.

"Oliver," she called, pausing to catch her breath. "Come out. *Immediately.*"

He didn't move.

"I had had enough of your games, Oliver," she said firmly.

Her gaze caught on the stall opposite her. She jumped back as a wild looking stallion peered back at her, pawing the ground with his massive hoof. Charlotte retreated another step, eyes on the mighty hooves visible beneath the half-stall door. The beast flattened its ears and tossed its head, letting out a vicious snort to announce its unhappiness with her presence.

Charlotte inched along the wall toward Oliver's stall, hissing, "It's dangerous here, Oliver. We must go now."

Still, the boy refused to answer.

The stallion whinnied again.

Charlotte drew a shaky breath. "You're such a lovely horse," she crooned, inching past and added wryly, "Whatever are you afraid of, Charlotte? The animal is locked safely in its stall."

The horse continued to snort and paw the ground, as it watched her every move. Gathering courage, she scurried to Oliver's stall only to discover the green hat dangling on the handle of a pitchfork.

"*What the devil?*" Charlotte snatched up the hat.

Giggles overhead made her look up. She froze. He scampered among the low rafters. Low, but not low enough for her to reach up and drag him down by a leg.

"Come down, at once." She gasped when he leapt from beam to beam. "It's far too dangerous, Oliver! Whatever are you thinking?"

He jumped to the beam over the stallion's stall and balanced on the rafter, looking down at her with a devious glint of mischief—then his eyes widened and his arms flailed.

He fell.

Charlotte lunged toward the stall and yanked the latch. The stallion screamed and reared, its massive front hooves slicing the air. Then it charged her. Strong hands seized her arm and yanked her out of the stallion's path, and into the opposite stall, as more horses galloped past. She stumbled and fell, landing hard under a muscled chest as the stallion thundered past. Men's voices rang out.

Overhead, Oliver scrambled into the safety of the rafters.

Charlotte closed her eyes in relief. When she opened them again, she came face-to-face with Lord Cassilis who lay on top of her, his green eyes inches from hers. Her heart thundered.

His mouth thinned in a grim line. "That stallion is wild, Miss Atchenson." A strand of dark hair fell over his face. "It's dangerous."

Suddenly, Charlotte became aware of the rugged planes of his chest and the weight of his body. Her breath caught. His lashes lowered. Time slowed and the hectic voices around them faded. Slowly, he lifted a hand and traced the outline of her jaw with the pad of his thumb. Each gentle sweep sent fire coursing through her. She shifted her gaze to his mouth and the sensual dent of his chiseled chin. With his heavily fringed lashes riding low over his eyes, he bent his head until his lips hovered above hers.

A man's urgent voice shattered the spell.

"My lord! My lord!"

Charlotte froze. As Lord Cassilis began to rose, a soft moan of loss escaped her lips before she could bite it back. He hesitated and pinned her with a hungry look that stole her breath. He abruptly pushed to his feet, pulling her up with him. He put a finger to his lips and motioned for her to remain out of view in the stall, then stepped into the walkway, half within her view.

"Ah, my lord," said a voice she recognized as the same man who had called for Lord Cassilis. "It appears as if someone unlatched every one of the stall doors."

"Indeed." Alistair looked at the rafter where Oliver sat, hugging his knees, white-faced.

Lord Cassilis returned his gaze to the man. "And the horses?"

"Och, they've not gone far, my lord, even the stallion," the man replied. "We'll have them back soon enough."

"Very well," Alistair dismissed the man with a nod. Bootfalls receded as Lord Cassilis strode to where Oliver perched over the stall opposite Charlotte. He pointed at the stable floor. "Down. Now."

The boy dropped down at once.

"You could very well have gotten Miss Atchenson killed," Alistair said in a quiet voice.

The boy's face crumpled.

"This very morning, I treated you with kindness," Alistair's deep baritone continued. "Perhaps you would understand a whip better?"

Oliver paled.

A tense silence descended. Charlotte hurried from the stall to join them.

Alistair glanced at her, then pointed to the door and said to the boy, "Off with you to the nursery. I will discuss your punishment after supper, but you may start by adding another chapter of Latin to this morning's task. *Go.*"

Oliver ran.

Alistair faced her. "Charlotte, what were you doing in the line? Did Lady Cassilis bid you stand with the servants?"

She started at the unexpected question as well as the casual use of her name. He stood too close. So close, she felt the heat radiating from his body.

She dropped her gaze to the ground and replied, "I fear I have upset her, my lor—"

"Hush." He pressed a finger to her lips.

She froze.

His dark lashes dipped as his gaze locked on her mouth, then his hand fell away. "I weary of curtsies and 'my lords'." His eyes met hers and she started at the stark honesty. "You asked me once if you could call me Alistair. Indeed, I would prefer it."

Images collided in her head—the conversation in the library, the whisky, her moan on the stable floor.

"I-I must go." She gathered her skirts and fled.

. . .

He didn't follow. For that, Charlotte was grateful. Minutes later, she burst into the nursery, startling Meg where she sat at the table with the children.

"Losh, Miss, what's happened?" The jolly, freckle-faced maid jumped to her feet.

In an effort to regain her composure, Charlotte slowly closed the door then turned to face her. "Nothing's happened, Meg."

A speculative light leapt into Meg's eyes, but Charlotte ignored it and joined Oliver at the table, a broken quill in his hand and ink-blotted paper before him. She sat in the chair to his right.

"I have been trying to teach him his letters," Meg said as she left the table. "But you will do better, Miss. Jane and I are on our way to the kitchens."

Charlotte smiled and watched the little girl skip alongside Meg as the two of them disappeared through the door before returning her attention to Oliver.

"Will he beat me?" Oliver asked in a soft voice.

Charlotte noticed his white knuckled grip on the quill.

"I fear you might deserve it," she replied. "Someone might have been killed."

He blanched. "I…didn't think…"

Her heart tugged and she smoothed his dark hair away from his forehead. "Let's cross that bridge when we come to it." She opened the Latin grammar to the first page. "Your father only wishes you to become a fine, upstanding gentleman. Now, concentrate on your task." She patted the paper. "Come, let's start."

Oliver took a deep, quavering breath and nodded.

By the end of the hour, over a dozen broken quills littered the table's surface, but Charlotte was pleased with the boy's perseverance. He licked his lips as he stubbornly scratched the unknown shapes. Very little was legible, but she didn't think Alistair would mind.

A smile played over her lips for a good five minutes before she realized she was behaving like a fool. Really, Charlotte! Alistair? *Alistair?* Since *when* had he become *Alistair* and not Lord Cassilis?

She rose and busied herself with reorganizing the supplies in the cupboard. After a time, Meg and Jane returned with an early dinner of stewed fowl, barley-broth, and a cranberry-tart with a rich cream sauce. By the time they'd finished the meal, darkness had fallen and Oliver's mood—as well as Charlotte's —had lightened. The maid had just left with the dishes when a sudden keening wail in the castle below caused them all—with the exception of Meg—to jump.

"Whatever is that sound?" Charlotte looked at Meg, who sat in her chair near the fire.

"Och, it's just the piper, lass," the red-haired maid laughed. When they all looked confused, she rose from her chair near the fire and went to the door. "It's Foster. He used to play the pipes every night afore the evening meal, but he's been a wee tired of late. But tonight, with the guests..." She opened the door. "Come, come." She waved them out of the nursery. "I'll show you."

Fascinated, Charlotte took each child by the hand and followed her into the hall. Night had fallen and the dim light of the candles added mystery to the mournful lilt filtering up the stairs as they walked toward the grand staircase.

"Losh, you should see his kilt," Meg whispered when they reached the staircase. "'Tis a sight to see. He is just down the next level. We can be down and back in a flash, before anyone knows. They are all in the dining room by now."

"Can we?" Oliver tugged Charlotte's hand.

Jane chimed in and Meg waggled pleading brows. Charlotte

gave in. After all, it was their heritage. "Only for a minute," she whispered back.

She led the way, tiptoeing down the red-carpeted steps. They reached the second floor, which, thankfully, was empty, and Charlotte waved everyone forward. The pipe played on as they knelt and peered between the columns at Foster. He paced before the bottommost step, playing the pipes, magnificent in his green pleated kilt, broad leather belt and wool doublet jacket.

As the children watched, mesmerized, Charlotte closed her eyes and let the lament, wild and plaintive, wash over her in gentle reminder that she no longer lived in England. The last notes of the song faded, she rose to her feet, and reached for the children's hands.

"What are you doing here?" Lady Cassilis's voice broke the spell.

Charlotte whirled. The woman stood two feet away, wearing a light green-striped evening dress with a wide, square neckline adorned with blue velvet ribbon. A beautiful young, honey-haired woman hovered by her side, her dress an elegant ivory color trimmed in pearls that perfectly complemented the silver and pearl tiara woven into her thick, lustrous hair. They both looked so elegant, so refined that Charlotte suddenly felt like a dowdy hen in the presence of two majestic swans.

"I repeat, what are you doing here?" Lady Cassilis's eyes flicked over her disdainfully. "Servants are not to be seen near the grand staircase. You have your own stairs."

"Pardon me, my lady," Charlotte dropped a curtsey. "The children merely wished to hear the piper."

"Do we indulge a child's every whim?" She snapped opened her fan. "Especially, the children of a beggar woman?"

"My ma was a fine *lady*," Oliver said in a fierce voice. "Not a shrew, like you." Everyone, including Charlotte, gasped, and he quickly tacked on a "my lady" to lessen his sin.

Recovering first, Charlotte rounded on him. "Oliver! Apologize at once."

"Let me have a look at you." Lady Cassilis stepped forward, then put a finger under his chin and tilted his head from side to side. "Cassilis eyes, but nothing else."

Oliver jerked his head out of her grasp and clenched his hands into fists. "I'll not apologize. *No* one insults my mum."

Lady Cassilis reeled back in shock. "The uncouth urchin! Dare he speak to me so?" She whirled on Charlotte. "Is not a governess to teach *manners*? Or is that something—"

"Manners?" a deep baritone voice cut in.

Charlotte looked up. Alistair stood at the top of the stairs.

Lady Cassilis began to fan her face. "It is the dinner hour, I see." Looking at the young lady by her side, she added, "Shall we, my dear?"

As she lifted her chin and headed for the descending stairs, Charlotte heaved a breath of relief and grasped Oliver by the arm, intending to make a run for the nursery.

"Miss Atchenson," Lord Cassilis called. "If you will join me in the library?"

Charlotte glanced over to find his gaze already locked on her.

Lady Cassilis paused and looked over her shoulder at him. "It is the dinner hour, Alistair. Polite society requires that one not keep guests waiting."

He lifted a cool brow. "I daresay you look well-fed enough to wait another quarter of an hour, Lady Cassilis. If ye feel faint, please have tea and biscuits served in the drawing room."

Her mouth dropped open.

He nodded to Oliver. "And I'll see you as well, lad. Come, the both of you."

He strode down the hall, leaving Charlotte and Oliver to hurry after him. A moment later, Charlotte stood with Oliver before the library fire. She laid a hand on the boy's thin shoulder and gave him a reassuring squeeze as his father crossed to the sideboard. When he reached for the flask of whisky, she winced.

She dropped a curtsey. "My lord, I fear I have offended Lady Cassilis—"

"Don't give the woman one scrap of attention, Charlotte," he interjected quietly as he poured the whisky into a glass. "I would be far more concerned if she should like you."

Charlotte blinked.

He turned, glass of whisky in hand, and extended it toward her. She frowned, then glimpsed the gleam of amusement lurking in his expressive eyes.

"Care for a drink?" A trace of a smile edged his mouth.

She narrowed her eyes. "Not tonight, my lord."

With a wink, he leaned a hip against the sideboard and looked at Oliver. "I was of a mind to thrash you soundly, lad," he began in a deep, solemn tone, "for your mischief in the stables."

"I'm sorry," Oliver squeaked.

"Aye," his father replied. "But being sorry doesn't prevent someone from being hurt."

The boy ducked his head and nodded.

"You must show respect," Alistair continued in a firm voice. "You've no cause to insult a lady, even one as venomous as Lady Cassilis, and you ignored Miss Atchenson. Did she not ask you to apologize?"

Oliver's head bowed lower.

"However, you stood up for your mother's good name, and against an old harridan of a witch as well, lad. That takes courage."

Charlotte blinked. Oliver's head snapped up.

"A man must protect those in his care." Alistair's stern features relaxed. "As a man of the Cassilis clan, I'll see you look after your mother's good name and your governess as well. But if you get into such mischief again, I'll thrash you soundly —*then* lock you in with Lady Cassilis for a week."

The boy turned white.

Charlotte suppressed a smile. Perhaps the man wasn't a bad father, after all. He sipped his whisky and her gaze snagged on the way his coat went taut across his shoulders. Her mouth went dry. How was it possible for a man to be so handsome?

"How is your Latin?" he asked.

Charlotte jarred.

Oliver's eyes widened and, when he didn't reply, Charlotte said, "He is laboring faithfully, my lord."

His eyes slicked to the boy's ink-stained cuffs. "I see. Then you may go, Oliver. Goodnight."

The boy bowed.

The door to the library opened and Alistair's raven-haired friend, Nicholas, entered. A broad grin lit his face. "Ah, Alistair, care to intro—"

"You may leave, Miss Atchenson," Alistair cut the man off. He strode to the door, held it wide and jerked his head at the hallway beyond.

The curt gesture made her wonder at his sudden change of mood. But grateful to escape without further recrimination, she caught Oliver's hand and hurried with him out the door. Lord Cassilis clicked the door firmly shut behind her. She glanced back, then shook off her confusion and faced forward.

Oliver's fingers tightened around hers and she was startled to realize he hadn't pulled free. "You're a fortunate boy, Oliver. Let's see you stay out of mischief, shall we?"

To her surprise, he cracked a grin and nodded. Charlotte smiled back. Maybe the boy was starting to settle in.

"Why don't you run on ahead to the nursery?" she coaxed. She needed a few minutes alone.

"Should I start on my Latin?" he asked.

"Exactly," she said.

Without another word, he scampered off toward the back stairs.

Charlotte followed at a slower pace. She knew she shouldn't dwell on Alistair, but how could she not? The more she grew to know him, the more she thought him an honorable man. The thought gave her pause. How strange that such a man would abandoned his children to begin with.

"Charlotte?"

Lord Cassilis was kind and he cared how the children were raised. Why—

"Charlotte?" a male voice said again.

She stopped.

"Charlotte?" the voice repeated in wonder.

Her heart began to pound. She knew that voice. Charlotte whirled. He stood at the end of the hallway. He looked the same, the reddish-brown beard, the chilling blue eyes. She even recognized the blue waistcoat with silver buttons.

"Charlotte?" Captain Edwards started toward her. "Whatever are you doing here?"

CHAPTER 8

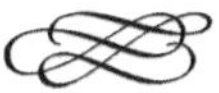

Charlotte stared at Captain Edwards in complete shock.
What was *he* doing here?

"It really is you." The Captain reached her, grabbed her arm, and yanked her aside. "How did you know to find me here? I'm not giving you a penny. We are finished."

Charlotte stared with her mouth flopped open like a fish. His hand tightened on her arm. She jerked her gaze onto his fingers, then yanked free.

"Do not touch me. Devil knows I would never follow you. This is my place of employment."

"Employment?" He frowned. "You hold a position *here*?"

"Do not pretend that hardened shell you call a heart cares what position I hold." Charlotte lunged past him toward the servants' stairs.

Oliver met her at the bottom step. "Who's that man?" He leaned to look behind her.

She grasped his arm and pulled him up the stairs after her. "A bad man," she replied. "The kind of man you should never be."

By the time they entered the nursery, she shook with anger.

The *arrogance* of the man. What a small mind he had—that he should think she followed him. And for what? Ten more shillings?

Charlotte ordered Oliver to remove his ink-stained shirt and went to fetch his bedclothes from his room. When she returned, she found him seated cross-legged before the fire, turning the pages of the Latin grammar book with decided interest.

The sight calmed her raging thoughts and she knelt beside him. "Tomorrow, we will work on your letters," she promised. "Soon, you'll be able to copy both chapters." He nodded and smiled back, a genuine smile that lit his small face. Not wanting to spoil the moment, she jostled his nightshirt over his head, saying, "Now, off to bed. We will begin your lessons tomorrow."

"Yes, Miss," he muttered as his head emerged. He leapt to his feet and scampered toward his room. He paused at the door to say in a gruff voice, "Goodnight, Miss."

Charlotte nodded in reply and watched him disappear into his room, still hugging the book to his chest. After checking on Meg and Jane, she escaped to her own room and plopped down on the bed.

Her thoughts returned at once to Captain Edwards. Had he been invited to Lord Cassilis's party? It hadn't occurred to her the two men might be friends. She drew a sharp breath. What if the Captain convinced Lord Cassilis that hiring Charlotte had been a mistake?

CHARLOTTE SPENT THE ENSUING DAYS BEHAVING AS A PROPER governess should. She found the guidance in *The Fine Art of Deportment* dull, and could scarcely finish a page without yawning.

Mornings, she taught Oliver his letters and Jane how to draw. Afternoons, she took the children for walks about the estate, exploring the terraced gardens, orchards, the ice house and Swan Pond. Twice they explored the shore near the old sea caves, which were-carved into the face of the cliff upon which the castle perched.

Several times, she caught sight of Lord Cassilis in the distance, mounted on a splendid bay as he escorted his guests around the estate. He sat with ease in the saddle. Despite the distance, he cut a dashing figure, and was far more handsome than the other men in his party. Which was probably why the beautiful young woman she'd seen hovering behind Lady Cassilis chose to ride alongside him. Charlotte tried to ignore the pangs of jealousy. Lady Cassilis was right. Charlotte was born to clean the Blue Drawing Room, not sit in it.

Once or twice, she spied Captain Edwards galloping behind Alistair. So, he was Lord Cassilis's guest for the duration of the party. Was the Captain's presence why his lordship hadn't spoken with her since his guests had arrived? That was as it should be, but the knowledge didn't halt the fear.

Two days after spotting Lord Cassilis riding with his guests, Charlotte and the children descended the cliff to explore the Dolphin House, the crowstepped, gabled laundry nestled on the shore. The children, with forlorn expressions, watched the women work, the tubs and atmosphere clearly reminding them of their mother. Noticing their wistful expressions, the laundresses invited them to help.

"You can, too, Miss Atchenson," a wizened laundress with a gap-toothed smile waved for her to join in while she filled a large, wooden tub. "What more fun can be had than to spend a day filling the tubs?" She followed the comment with a sarcastic eye roll, then cast a look of wonder at the children willingly lugging buckets of water from the shore.

"I thank you for the offer, but no," Charlotte declined with a laugh.

She stayed for a time, but when the children asked to stay longer and the laundress waved her away, she wandered up the shore toward the old sea caves.

Large boulders framed the path leading up to a ruined arched doorway chiseled into the bedrock, which marked the entrance to an ancient shelter hewn within the caverns. Moss-covered rocks dominated the landscape, and dry vines clawed up the cliff face and wove through abandoned windows. She picked her way over the boulders and peered into the main abandoned chamber. Wind whistled through the ruined windows above. Beach pebbles covered the damp floor, pools of water scattered here and there. Suddenly uneasy, she ducked out of the cave and stepped around a large boulder. At the sound of voices mingling in angry tones, she froze.

"You promised delivery," a woman railed. "All I *ever* get from you are demands for more coin."

Charlotte knew that female voice. Cautiously, she peered around the boulder. Lady Cassilis stood a short distance away, wind whipping her skirts as she spoke to a thin, bulging-eyed man with a pockmarked face, thick eyebrows, and greasy hair. His stained shirt and worn breeches flapped against his tall, lanky frame.

As Charlotte watched, Lady Cassilis withdrew a small leather bag from a pocket in her skirts and tossed it at the man. He caught it with a deft maneuver and hefted it in his hand. A smile split his lips. Suddenly, he glanced in Charlotte's direction. His thick eyebrows arched as he blinked in surprise. Lady Cassilis whirled, following his line-of-sight.

Charlotte gulped when Lady Cassilis's face contorted into a mask of anger. Charlotte whirled. Yanking up her skirts, she raced down the path to the Dolphin House. What was going on? No lady conducted clandestine meetings with disreputable men. What would Lord Cassilis think of this? Charlotte's side began to ache. She glanced back. No one chased her. She slowed, breathing hard, but kept at a fast walk.

Should she tell Lord Cassilis what she'd seen? No. Lady Cassilis would deny it, and he would likely turn out Charlotte without a reference. By the time she pushed open the door to the castle laundry, the stitch in her side had disappeared, but her nerves were frazzled.

Heart still pounding, she collected the children and hurried back to the castle with the promise of extra biscuits for their afternoon tea. They ran up the path, one dark head, one red, as Charlotte followed. They'd no sooner crossed the castle lawn and arrived at the kitchen door when a maid shaking a sheet from a window above called down, "Best hurry, Charlotte. The dressmaker's been waiting, lass."

Charlotte frowned, puzzled, but nodded her thanks as she herded the children up the servant stairs and into the nursery. Dressmaker?

They entered the nursery and Charlotte noted the three large, iron-banded trunks stacked next to a slight, middle-aged woman with prematurely white hair, a pointed chin, and warm brown eyes who perched on a three-legged stool. The children hurried to the trunks and began to examine them.

"What's all this?" Charlotte asked.

"Losh, the trunks are for you, Miss," Meg exclaimed. "Day dresses, evening dresses, and a ball gown, as well."

Charlotte looked at her, confused, and the woman rose spryly to her feet. "I am the dressmaker, my dear, and I am *delighted* to meet you, Miss Atchenson." She crossed to Charlotte, then grasped her hands, lifting and spreading them wide. "Now, twirl in a circle for me." Charlotte didn't move and the woman grasped her shoulder and turned her. "What a fine figure you have." She clucked her tongue in admiration. "We shall dress you like a *queen*."

Charlotte pulled free and said, "I am no queen, madam. I am the governess. I feel certain the children are your clients. There's been a misunderstanding."

"Fanny, my dear. Please call me Fanny," the woman quickly replied, her eyes crinkling in the corners. "And, yes, there does indeed seem to be a misunderstanding, but it's not mine. Lord Cassilis did hire me to sew the children's wardrobes. Their trunks are in their rooms

"That was Lord Cassilis's doing?" Charlotte murmured. So, the man had taken her reprimand in the carriage to heart.

Fanny shot her a look. "He was quite adamant that I sew full wardrobes for both of them. I and my seamstress didn't sleep a wink, I tell you." She laughed and shook her head, then her expression shifted. "I have also been paid to sew a ball gown and all the rest—not children's clothing. And not just any ball gown, my dear, but a most bonny one." She hurried to the trunks and unclasped the lid of the one on top. When she tipped it up, Charlotte froze as crimson silk spilled from the chest.

"I would have been here much sooner." The dressmaker touched the material to her withered cheek. "But it took some doing to find this particular shade. Such a lovely color." She set the cloth aside, then pulled a length of crimson brocade from another trunk. "We will sew a sumptuously elegant, dainty creation, my dear, and we'll trim the puffed sleeves with this brocade, as well as pearls, netting lace, and ribbon—"

"Crimson?" Charlotte finally managed to say.

Fanny gathered the material back into the trunk and shut the lid. "Lord Cassilis expressly asked for crimson silk."

Lord Cassilis? Charlotte blinked. A crimson ball gown? *How had he known?* "It must be an error," she said. It had to be—or else she'd divulged *much* more that night in the library than she'd thought she had. She winced at the idea.

Fanny's sharp brown eyes smiled. "Much more than a ball

gown, child. His lordship has commissioned me to supply your wardrobe, as well. I am to sew morning, visiting, and walking gowns, a riding habit and stockings, spencers, a pelisse for each—"

"*The devil, no—*" Charlotte swore, then clamped a hand over her mouth in wide-eyed embarrassment.

The dressmaker and Meg laughed. Even Oliver grinned wickedly.

Charlotte grimaced and lifted a warning finger at him. "My mistake is no excuse to not mind your tongue," she warned, then faced the dressmaker once again.

The woman cut her off before she could say more. "You are welcome to ask his lordship, as you please. When I spoke with him earlier, he mentioned you might object. Told me to tell you to come right down to the library. I imagine he's still there, love."

Charlotte's heart began to pound. She'd been trying to avoid him. She hesitated. "I shall be quick," she promised, then left.

Minutes later, she stood before the library's solid oak door. With a critical gaze over her blue gown, she smoothed her skirts and scowled at the frayed hem. Yes, she sorely needed clothes, but serviceable items, and, most definitely, not a ball gown—and a crimson one at that. She flinched. Crimson? *Had she told the man her every secret?*

"Enough, Charlotte." She bit her lower lip to steel her resolve and knocked sharply on the door.

It opened before the third rap. Charlotte blinked. Lord Cassilis stood on the threshold as handsome as ever in a white, puffed-sleeve linen shirt with an ivory waistcoat and a pair of dark gray trousers.

"Miss Atchenson." The low timbre of his voice turned her insides to jelly. He stepped back and he waved her in. "Come in. What a delight to see you, at last."

"My lord." She curtsied, then entered.

He shut the door, then faced her. "You have been avoiding me of late."

"Not at all, my lord." The lie sounded gruff and false, even to her own ears. "The seamstress is under the impression that she is to sew a wardrobe for me and—"

"She is," he cut in with a smile.

Charlotte paused. The warmth of that smile could melt the coldest of hearts. She cleared her throat. "My lord, it is too much—"

"Let me be the judge of that," he interrupted again.

Sacre-bleu. It was hard not to drown in those green eyes. She drew a deep breath. "What use could they possibly be, my lord? I have no need of riding habits and most certainly not a ballgown." Especially a crimson one.

"I beg to differ. As a governess in my employ, you represent my house, do you not?"

She nodded.

"Then you must dress the part."

Damn the man, he seemed too pleased with himself.

"Then a serviceable dress or two, at most, my lord." She smoothed her hands a bit self-consciously over her dress. "I am a governess. I have no use for such a wardrobe."

His gaze caught and held hers. She was the first to glance away.

"Aye, you are a governess," he murmured.

She hazarded a look at him. His eyes locked with hers again. This time, she didn't look away. Keeping her distance and acting like a governess wasn't going at all as she'd planned—but as she searched his compelling green gaze, only one question truly burned her soul.

"Why crimson?" she breathed.

His eyes glittered. "Why not?"

She tried to clear her thoughts, but he mesmerized her as if he'd cast a spell. His eyes dropped to her mouth. What were they speaking of? Ah, the dress.

She cleared her throat. "It is a rather…scandalous gown… far too bold to represent a noble house…and…" Her voice trailed away and all at once, the day's growth of beard darkening his strong jaw seemed much more pleasant to ponder.

"Nonsense," he disagreed. "With your hair and those eyes, a crimson gown would be stunning on you."

She felt herself melt into the warmth of his eyes. Her heart began to pound. He stepped closer. From the rise and fall of his chest, she knew he was going to kiss her—and that she'd let him if she stayed. Such a thing was far too dangerous, a Pandora's Box that should never be opened. Charlotte darted around him and took a step toward the door.

He caught her wrist. "Stay."

"I cannot," she whispered.

Charlotte threw the door open and flew down the hallway. She skirted the grand oval staircase only to collide with a hard body stepping out from behind a marble column. She stumbled back, but a heavy hand clamped down on her shoulder.

Captain Edwards.

He pulled her roughly against his chest.

"Unhand me!" Charlotte twisted in an attempt to wrench free.

The Captain's fingers tightened on her shoulders. "You are a credit to your father—or what he once was."

Her jaw dropped. The *audacity* of the man. "You have no right to speak of my father. Let me go."

His hold tightened. "I worry for you, Charlotte, cast adrift in this place."

"You worry *now?*" she retorted. "Why not in London, when I desperately needed your help?" She choked, too angry to continue, and shoved his chest harder.

"We shouldn't quarrel, Charlotte." A hungry gleam entered his eyes.

Fear slammed into her. She wriggled, but he only crushed her tighter.

"I miss you, Charlotte." He dropped his head, his beard grazing her neck. "I need you." He groaned.

Disgust rolled over her. Hadn't she already escaped the man? Was he trying to drag her back? "I will never marry you," she swore.

He straightened and laughed. "I could never *marry* you. But I will accept you as my mistress. You must be discreet." He splayed his fingers low on her hip.

Her stomach turned. "You arrogant fool. I want nothing to do with you. I *never* did, and I *never* will."

The dinner gong sounded.

Voices sounded on the staircase, from levels above and below. The Captain's hold loosened as he glanced over his shoulder. She shoved at his chest, then froze when movement down the hall caught her eye.

Lord Cassilis turned the corner and froze.

Before Charlotte could react, a woman's voice called nearby, "Captain?"

The Captain jerked away, and as guests flooded the hall, blocking her view of Lord Cassilis as, she turned on her heel and marched away, regretting she hadn't had the chance to knee Captain Edwards in the groin.

CHAPTER 9

ALISTAIR FORCED HIS FEET TO CARRY HIM TOWARD THE DINING room. Primal jealousy burned in his veins. He would never forget the image of Charlotte in Captain Edwards' arms. The image scorched his brain. She'd told him of her engagement. Could Captain Edwards be *the* captain she'd spoken of? What were the odds? Had the man discovered her missing in London and sought her out? What man would allow his fiancée to fall into such dire straits that she must take on a position as governess?

Those questions swirled in Alistair's mind, each leaving him in a darker mood than the last, as he took his seat at the head of the table. The dinner guests filed past him, but he had eyes only for the captain as he sat and the dinner began.

The women on each side of Alistair attempted to draw him into conversation, but he retained only vague impressions of their faces and heard little of what they said. What could Charlotte admire in such a man? He clearly lacked ethics, and was weak-chinned to boot. The thought of her kissing such a dolt twisted his gut.

As the dinner progressed, Alistair downed his wine

untasted and sifted through his recollections of the past week for any information about the man. They'd once exchanged brief words in the library over glasses of claret, and once again during an afternoon ride on the estate. Beyond that, he hadn't paid the pompous core much attention. Now, he couldn't take his eyes off that smug face.

What the *deuce* did Charlotte see in him?

As if sensing Alistair's stare, Captain Edwards looked up and nodded politely his way.

It was an opening. "How might you know Miss Atchenson, Captain?" Alistair raised his voice above the din.

The voices around the dinner table quieted.

Edwards coughed loudly. "I, uh, have…heard of…uh, her through mutual friends, my lord."

Heard? An odd way to speak of one's fiancée. "Are you not, at least, acquaintances, Captain?"

The guests swiveled their heads back to the captain.

The man turned red. "Nae, no. Not really. Not at all."

Odd. Alistair narrowed his eyes. Exceedingly odd.

The guests began to whisper.

The captain fixed his eyes intently on his plate.

Alistair frowned. What manner of man denied his engagement? Or…was their connection a clandestine affair? Charlotte wasn't that kind of a woman. Hell, she'd practically fled his company. *Twice.* Perhaps the captain had led her on with false hope? He expelled a derisive snort at the thought, only to become aware of a strained silence and his guests' stares.

Nicholas' voice rose, "What are the forthcoming plays in Edinburgh this summer?"

The buzz in the dining room resumed.

Cutlery clinked. Voices buzzed. Courses came and went.

Alistair didn't know what he ate. He couldn't prevent his gaze from straying to the captain, to note every minute detail—how his head bobbed, and the nasal quality of his laugh.

At last, the final course was served. Alistair waited long enough for the lady on this right to finish the last of her cake, then he rose, signaling that the blasted dinner had reached its morbid end.

As the ladies retired to the Blue Drawing Room, he headed to the library with the men, keenly aware that the captain followed at his heel. Within ten minutes of standing by the fire, nursing his claret, Alistair could no longer bear another moment of the man's nasally laugh.

"If you will excuse me, gentlemen." He set his claret on the sideboard and strode from the room without further explanation.

He'd nearly reached his study when Nicholas caught up with him.

"Ho there, lad." His friend matched his stride. "Are you ill?"

Alistair exhaled in irritation. "Captain Edwards is an ass."

"A dull fellow, to be sure," Nicholas replied with a snort of amusement.

Alistair cast him a narrow-eyed glare, but made no reply. They reached the study, his private haven from the gilded luxury of the castle. He rubbed the back of his neck, eyeing the two simple brown wingback chairs, the table with its candlestick, the simple whisky cupboard and the fireplace. What else did a man need?

Nicholas lit a taper from the fire in the hearth as Alistair strode to the cupboard. He poured two glasses of whisky, gave one to his friend, then sat down heavily in the empty chair.

Nicholas sipped of whisky, then asked, "What has Captain Edwards to do with your bonny governess?"

Alistair tossed him a suspicious look. "Why speak of her?"

"Why ask the man, at the dinner table, if he knew her?" Nicholas asked in turn.

Ah, that. Alistair shrugged.

His friend laughed. "'Tis plain as day, you're besotted with the lass."

Alistair sipped his drink. Why deny it? "She has a fiancé. A feckless fop of a man."

Nicholas laughed again. "Not the hapless Captain Edwards? Oh, that is interesting." He tossed back the rest of his whisky, then set the glass on the table and rose. "As ever, my friend, you choose the harder path. But I've yet to see you fail. With that, I bid you a good night." Halfway to the door, he halted and turned. "Ah, Lady Cassilis."

Alistair shifted his attention to the right and met Nicholas' eyes.

"I swear I saw her in Maidens today," Nicholas said. "In the company of a strange man—a working man, and not very skilled, judging by his appearance."

"A man?" Alistair echoed, mildly surprised. "That is strange." She held her reputation dear. She wouldn't allow herself to be seen with a strange man, especially one of the working-class.

"I find her riding in a fishing village even stranger," Nicholas said. "Surely, the proof she claims to have discovered cannot be found there."

The woman had yet to confront him. Alistair shrugged. "Until she plays her hand, I have no way of knowing what she's up to. I can do nothing but wait."

"*Wait.*" Nicholas shuddered. "I detest the word."

Alistair grunted a laugh.

"Who can fathom how that woman's mind works, eh?"

Alistair didn't answer.

Nicholas bade him good night, strode out the door, and shut it behind him.

Alistair took another swig of whisky. He needed to discover how Lady Cassilis planned to contest his legitimacy—later. For the moment, he had more pressing matters to deal with. Memory rose of Charlotte in her captain's embrace.

Nicholas was right. He wouldn't retreat. He'd choose the harder path.

He lifted his whisky and watched the flames of the fire reflecting in its depths. He absolutely would not let Charlotte wed the scoundrel.

ALISTAIR AROSE THE NEXT MORNING WITH A RARE HEADACHE. He'd spent a sleepless night puzzling just how he might open Charlotte's eyes and still had yet to settle on a plan. He entered the breakfast parlor in a dark mood. Guests came and went. Some greeted him with nods before he responded with a scowl, which sent them scurrying. He would have to remember to glower more often. After washing the last of his eggs down with a cup of tea, he escaped to the stables, saddled his favorite roan, and rode out onto his estate, his mind still on Charlotte.

Heavy dark clouds hung on the horizon as he cantered past the orchards and south into the forest beyond. Spring would arrive soon. Already, the first hint of buds dusted the branches of the hawthorn and silver birch dotting the rolling hills. He closed his eyes and breathed deeply of the brisk morning air. The land sang in his blood. In all his travels, he had yet to find a place better than Culzean, the seat of his clan. He'd poured every penny of his vast fortune into the estate.

He pondered his stepmother. She intended to prove him illegitimate, yet he'd seen nothing of her plan save once catching her in the library, poking through the musty pages of long ignored books. Why take so long to prove her case? With so many witnesses to his scandalous origins, surely proof of his illegitimacy wouldn't be hard to find. And what of her trip to the village of Maidens? He would have to ride there himself and see what he might discover—but, another day. Today, he intended to settle the matter of Charlotte.

He urged his horse east and trotted over rocky green hills and under trees. He'd have to spend more time with the lass in order to open her eyes to the captain's unsuitability. Why she would yoke herself to the man bewildered him mightily. She was such a cheeky lass and the man quite unworthy of her. Such a union would be a travesty. The more he thought on the matter, the more his irritation grew. By the time the first fat drops of rain began to fall, he found his headache had returned with a vengeance.

With a curse, he wheeled his horse and headed home. The rain intensified and, seeing Piper's Brae running through the trees ahead, he dug his heel in his horse's side. The beast broke into a gallop, sailed over a low line of shrubs and landed in the middle of the road.

A sudden movement to his left drew his attention. Through the downpour, he glimpsed a man wearing a green cap with a red feather tucked in the brim before he vanished into the trees near the Swan Pond. What the devil? Alistair started to urge his horse after the man, then thought better of it. The driving rain had already soaked him to the bone. Chasing a wanderer wasn't worth the chance of catching his death. He spurred his horse once again with a "Ho there," and headed home.

Minutes later, he galloped down the castle drive and under the arched entrance just in time to see a fine barouche roll to a stop before the castle doors. Thankfully, the rain had dwindled to a drizzle. He eyed the vehicle with a scowl. What fresh hell was this? Already, he found the house party beyond tiresome.

A man hopped from the carriage and with a broad smile, waved as Alistair cantered past, headed for the clock tower and stables. By the time he'd seen his horse settled and returned the way he had come, the wind and rain had driven the newly arrived guests inside. The fact he'd escaped the wearisome charade of greetings put him in a perversely good mood and, in an effort to keep it that way, he dashed to the back of the castle and entered through the kitchens.

"My lord!" the cook cried. "We didnae expect to see ye."

Apparently not, for the entire staff froze and stared like frightened rabbits.

He smiled. "Never fear, Madam, I am only passing through." He waved them back to their business and turned up the servants' stairs, taking the steps two at a time. He detoured first to his room for fresh, dry clothes, then resumed his ascent to the nursery.

At the sound of muffled laughter, he turned the handle and eased open the nursery door a crack until Charlotte came into view. She sat with the children at a table set for afternoon tea. His heart warmed at sight of the familial gathering. When he'd decided to take in his niece and nephew, it hadn't occurred to him that he might be starting a family. Duty dictated he care for his kin, and duty was as far as he'd gotten. It also hadn't occurred to him that he might fall in love—ever—much less with a woman in his employ. He couldn't fail to miss the parallel with his own parents' relationship.

As Charlotte smiled at Jane, his attention snagged on Charlotte's delicate jaw. He slid his gaze down the graceful line of her neck to the rise of her breasts above the blue muslin bodice. He drew his eyes up the line of her spine and locked his gaze on her recalcitrant curls. They clustered at the nape of her neck simply begged to be twisted around his fingers. As he watched, she tilted her head back, lifted her nose high, and held her tea cup high in the air with her pinky extended.

"One *sips* their tea, Oliver," she said in an overly exaggerated, prim-and-proper falsetto. "And one must *lift* the nose in disdain."

The children giggled.

Alistair bit back a laugh, delighted to have caught her in a playful mood.

"Say it again," the children urged. "Say it again."

"Speak softly, children," she urged in a hushed voice. Then, much to their delight, she lifted her nose again and mimicked a high-society lady's snooty drawl. "My deaaahhhh, *however* do you do?"

He pushed the door open a few inches more and caught sight of Meg, who sat by the fire. Her gaze met his and she opened her mouth, but he placed a finger to his lips and shook his head. She nodded, ever so slightly, and sent him a knowing smile.

"Pleaaaaase have a seat," Charlotte said in lofty tones. "Would you cahhhre for a drop of teaaaa?"

The children snickered. "More," they chorused. "More."

Charlotte laughed and, squinting into her teacup, set it on the table. "I fear there is no tea left. We drank it all."

"Losh, Charlotte, you don't need tea to make us laugh," Meg teased. "Do Lady Toffee Nose again, will you, now? I haven't laughed so hard in ages."

As Jane squealed and clapped her hands, Oliver leapt from his chair and, with the first real smile Alistair had seen on his small face, bowed and asked, "Lady Toffee Nose, may I have this dance?"

Charlotte lifted her nose so high in the air that a curl slipped free from her bun and coiled softly over her shoulder. How soft would her flesh feel beneath his lips? How would she taste? His body rushed with heat at the thought.

"But dancing might wrinkle my *fawwnncy* gown, my lord," Charlotte objected in her high-pitched, wobbly voice. She fanned her face with an imaginary fan. "And it mustn't be the waltz—such a *scandalous* dance. Let's dance a Scottish reel, but will you promise to mind my toes?"

"Nae," Oliver sniggered. "I shall step on them."

"Then, I shan't dance with you." She sniffed and waved her

imaginary fan again. "Besides, the musicians seem to have fallen asleep, do you not think so, Sir Oliver?"

Jane scrambled to her knees on the chair and began to sing. Meg joined in, clapping her hands to a rousing, jolly melody.

Again, Oliver bowed. "*Please*, Lady Toffee Nose."

She made him wait, drawing out the suspense, then finally said, "Very well."

Charlotte stood from the table and pranced to the center of the nursery where she curtseyed as Oliver bowed. They began to dance, laughing and twirling in a lively reel.

Charlotte looked so light on her feet, so carefree that Alistair found himself smiling, and when she twirled past him for the second time, he couldn't resist. As she spun, he pushed the door open and stepped inside. Alistair caught her about the waist abd swung her around until she stood in his arms, face to face.

She froze.

Jane's singing came to an abrupt end, but Meg's voice carried on a bit before melting into laughter.

Alistair looked down at Charlotte and smiled. "Shall we dance, Miss Atchenson?" He leaned closer. "Or should I say, Lady Toffee Nose?"

Charlotte stared, eyes wide and cheeks growing pink.

"That must be a yes." He pulled her close—much closer than propriety allowed—then cocked a brow at Meg and announced, "I, however, shall dance the waltz."

Charlotte tensed, but Meg gamely began to hum once again. The children joined in and he turned her in a twirl in time with the rhythm. She moved with perfect grace and fit so well against him. The top of her head just reached his chin. Wrapped in his arms, the perfume of her hair and the warmth of her body kindled a hot desire that made his body sing. He couldn't resist sliding his thumb an inch or two over the small of her back in an intimate gesture no one could see. Her head snapped up and he read in her eyes a combination of shy embarrassment and excitement. Aye, if she every fully unleashed that bold lass, he'd be powerless to resist her—but then, he already was.

After circling the nursery floor twice, he stopped.

She didn't immediately step away, but stared up at him, her lips parted. He saw the unspoken question in her eyes. She wanted to know his intention. He'd never wanted anything in his life as badly as to show her exactly what those intentions were, but now was neither the time nor place.

Instead, he lifted a brow and directed the conversation to safer ground. "Am I so frightening?" She frowned, and he added, "You look as though you've seen the ghostly piper, Charlotte."

She started and stepped out of his hold.

"The ghostly piper?" Oliver asked as Charlotte returned to her seat at the table and Jane climbed into Meg's lap in her chair near the hearth.

"Aye, the piper." Alistair tossed him a warm smile and went to the table. As he took his seat opposite Charlotte, he bumped a table leg, rattling the china.

Oliver skipped over to hop into the chair next to him. "A real ghost?" he asked.

"Aye, a real ghost." Alistair grinned. "On stormy days such as these, you will hear the skirl of his pipes on the wind. Listen." He put a finger to his lips and nodded at the window and the gray skies beyond.

The creak of Meg's rocker stopped and silence descended in the nursery as they held their breath so that only the gusts of wind battering the windowpanes could be heard.

After a few moments, Jane glanced uncertainly at him and Meg resumed her rocking.

Alistair resumed the tale. "It was years ago and on one such a day, that the Cassilis piper went for a wee wander into the cliff caves below the castle," he said in a low stage voice. "He took his dog and pipes along with him, wanting to play a good Scottish tune to banish the ghosts and evil spirits that had gathered in the caves. Only…" he let his voice trail away, then added in a whisper, "he never returned."

"Never?" Oliver breathed.

"Never," Alistair repeated in a lower, deeper voice.

It was too much for Jane. She squealed and buried her face in Meg's ample bosom. "There, there, lassie," the nursemaid chuckled, "it's only a tale."

"A tale to scare children." Charlotte sent him a chastising look.

The devil, but he wanted to kiss her.

With a playful wink that dared her to object, he lowered his voice even more, "Aye, wee children are frightened by the tale —and grown folk, as well."

At the wink, a fine blush crept up Charlotte's cheeks, but she lifted her chin and said, "Foolish folk."

The fire her eyes reignited the desire to taste her pink lips. The lass was too tempting.

"But the ghost—" Oliver was saying.

At Jane's whimper, Charlotte turned to the boy and scooped up a spoon, then brandished it in a mock threat. "Enough talk of such things. I'll rap the knuckles of the next person that mentions this piper and his ghosts."

How could he resist? Staring straight into her lovely hazel eyes, he leaned close to Oliver and said, "Aye, lad, the piper vanished…but his dog came back—shaking in fear and with not a hair left on his wee body."

Charlotte tossed her head. For a moment, he thought she'd back down, but to his great delight, she rapped the spoon across his knuckles. Alistair seized her hand. She tugged back, but he held her eyes. She parted her lips as if to speak, but only stared.

Understanding struck. She cared for him…just as he cared for her. The realization made his heart soar. He would reel her back from Edwards—he had to. No doubt, it would be a fine, intricate dance—but he was an excellent dancer. Slowly, he drew his hand away, letting her fingers slip through his. Only then, did he become aware of the others in the room, of Jane wailing and Meg shushing her as she lumbered to her feet.

"Losh, lassie, it's time for a wee nap," the nursery maid cajoled. "Let's leave these folk to their dreary tales." With a broad smile, she hefted Jane over her shoulder and carried her out of the room.

Oliver stood and leaned over the table. "The dog. Did its hair grow back?"

Alistair chuckled. He hadn't a clue, but he wasn't above embellishing the tale. "Aye, but it took a year or more."

"Will he play his pipes tonight?" Oliver cast a serious glance out the window.

"Och, now, he might, lad." Alistair laughed, then recalled the mysterious man in the forest. Alistair faced Charlotte. "I've seen you and the children wandering about in the afternoons. Have you come across a man wearing a green hat with a red feather near the Swan Pond?"

She blinked in surprise, but shook her head, "Nae, my lord."

Oliver sat back in his chair with a thump and fell silent.

The mood in the room had shifted. He sighed. The magic of the moment had fled. He should have known better. Suppressing another sigh, he rose.

Charlotte stood. "Thank your father for the tale, Oliver."

Father. He'd forgotten she thought him the wayward father. Of a certainty, she would be cautious with him, thinking him a scandalous rogue. But in this matter, Oliver came first. He couldn't deliver another blow to the lad in his current vulnerable state. Who knew what it would do to him to learn that his true father had abandoned him entirely. He looked at the lad's inscrutable face staring stoically ahead. Aye, he'd have to figure out just how to step into the role of 'father'—no matter how foreign the word felt.

Charlotte nudged Oliver's shoulder, but the boy shoved his chair back and ran from the room.

She started to follow, but Alistair caught her arm. "Time," he said softly. "The lad needs time."

She lifted her lashes, her brow furrowed. "He's an angry boy, my lord."

"Aye, he has every right to despise his ne'er-do-well father." Charles deserved nothing less.

Her lashes fluttered. "I must find him before he finds mischief." She dipped into a curtsey and disappeared into the boy's room.

Alistair sighed. She'd slipped through his fingers once again.

He left the nursery and reached the main floor when the dinner gong sounded, but the thought of sitting across the table from Captain Edwards curdled his appetite. Alistair ordered men to investigate the area around the Swan Pond, then decided to skip the evening meal altogether.

No doubt, such a scandalous act would entertain them all. Lady Cassilis and her ilk could retire to the Blue Drawing Room afterwards and engage in hours of salacious gossip over the nature of his disappearance and his failure to execute the duties of a good host. He let an acidic chuckle escape. Ah, they'd never see he had done his job right well for them. Truly, what more could a host *do* but provide the old biddies such an enchanting evening of gossip?

He entered the study and divested himself of his coat and vest and tossed them over the back of a chair. With a quick tug, he freed his cravat, then settled comfortably in his shirtsleeves near the fire.

His headache had vanished. No doubt, Charlotte had something to do with that—just as she had in giving him the blasted headache in the first place. He yawned, then leaned his head against the soft velvet of the chair and smiled. She'd fit so well against him, been so soft as they'd waltzed. And the teasing manner with which she'd rapped his knuckles with the spoon… If only she would let her true self out more often. Why did she hide herself? Had Captain Edwards played a role in that? Whatever the case, he would make her forget him. His blood stirred at the thought of just how he would make her forget.

Wind howled outside and rain pinged against the window-panes. He pictured Charlotte's pink lips and soft curves. He'd had his hands on the small of her back. What would her flesh feel like beneath his fingers? If he'd pulled her just a little closer, her breasts would have pressed against his chest. Desire wound through him. He relaxed, and pictured her, head bent back, rising on tiptoes to meet his mouth as he lowered his head to kiss her. Alistair closed his eyes. She would be so sweet…so very sweet…

A sharp knock on the door startled him awake. Bleary-eyed, he glanced at the clock on the mantle. Ten-thirty. Had he slept over an hour?

Another knock sounded. "Enter," he called.

The door opened and the old piper entered, his aged brows knotted with worry.

"What is it?" Alistair demanded.

"It's the laddie," he replied. "We have been searching every-where, but he's not been found. He may have left the castle."

Alistair started. "Oliver?"

The piper nodded and Alistair tossed a glance at the dark-ness outside the window. Recalling the lad's inordinate interest in the piper, he wondered if he'd venture out in such stormy weather.

"Bloody hell." He rose and headed for the door. "I'll lead a search of the cliffs and the shore." Alistair brushed past the piper and the older man fell in alongside as he strode down the hallway. They reached the grand staircase and descended to the main floor. "Send men to search the stables, and anywhere else the lad's been known to wander," Alistair ordered as they reached the last step.

A footman carrying a hooded, black oilskin cloak met him at the door, as another opened the outer castle doors. Alistair swirled the cloak over his shoulders as he crossed to the threshold. He squinted into the inky rage of the storm as men gathered behind him with oil lanterns.

The wind howled as he took a lantern from the nearest man and started forward. Pellets of rain stung his cheeks and wild gusts tore at his cloak as they made their way through the darkness toward the cliffs. The waves crashed against the rocks below and blasts of salty wind stung his nose. He and his men shouted Oliver's name, but in vain. The roaring winds ripped their voices from their throats and he feared the boy would never hear them, nor they him. The thought gave his step an extra urgency as he descended the slippery, rock-strewn path leading to the shore.

Once at the beach, they spread out over the rock pools. Alistair wiped rain from his face and studied the cave-pocked cliff rising dark and dangerous above them. Surely, the lad wouldn't go into the caves, especially on a night as this and after hearing the piper's tale. The winds whistled through the abandoned, crumbling arches like ethereal pipes playing in the night. Alistair raised his lantern and headed for the entrance when shouts from behind stopped him in his path.

The man reached them and shouted, "We found him, my lord."

Alistair strained to hear. "You found him?" he shouted back.

The man nodded. "In the castle." He said something else, but the words were drowned out by the wail of the wind and the pounding surf.

Relief flooded through Alistair, quickly followed by irritation. He hurried with his men up the path and through the castle doors to find himself cold and wet despite the oilskin cloak. As a footman peeled the garment off his back, Foster rushed forward to greet him.

Pushing back his wet hair, Alistair half growled, "Where is he?"

The old piper hesitated. "Charles' apartments, my lord."

Alistair paused. "Charles' apartments?" What was he doing *there?*

He caught sight of Edwards on the grand staircase above with other guests. With a scowl, Alistair strode down the corridor and headed for the rear stairs.

Minutes later, he donned a dry, white, loose-fitting linen shirt and a pair of gray trousers, then left his chambers for the finely decorated rooms that had served as his stepbrother's private apartments.

Candlelight spilled from the open bedroom doorway into the dimly lit hall. Alistair paused under the lintel, taking in the finely crafted four-poster bed, the settee, desk, armoire…and Charlotte.

She sat on the floor, knees drawn to her chest and her cheek resting against one knee, her attention on the boy curled up in the corner. Asleep on a pile of linens, Oliver clutched a large, full white laundress' apron tightly in his arms. Alistair's frustration melted away. The lad missed his mother.

Charlotte noticed him and started to rise, but he motioned her to remain seated. He approached softy, then knelt on one knee by her side and studied his young nephew. Odd the lad should find his father's room. Of all places, why had he run here?

With a sigh, he gently gathered the boy in his arms and carried him back to the nursery with Charlotte walking by his side in silence.

It wasn't until he laid the boy on his bed and drawn a blanket over his sleeping form that Charlotte began to apologize.

He shushed her with a finger on her lips. "You look fair exhausted, lass. Do no' fret. Get some sleep before our hellion awakes again."

She smiled, an unguarded smile that warmed his soul. His gaze dropped to her lips. He'd thought them so kissable from the start. For a moment, he almost reached out to trace the velvety softness with this thumb—but then, she'd reserved such intimate gestures for her fiancé.

Yet she cared for him. He'd seen it that evening.

Captain Edwards be damned.

He tucked a stray curl behind her ear. She tensed, but he bent down and pressed a kiss on her forehead. As she remained motionless, he stepped away, noting the pink flush on her cheeks.

He strode out the door, happier than he'd been in longer than he could remember.

CHAPTER 10

CHARLOTTE STOOD ROOTED TO THE SPOT, HER LIPS STILL burning from his touch. What was he doing to her? Their social positions set them worlds apart. He knew that. Why toy with her like this? He was tempting her because he was a man. Jane and Oliver were evidence of his rakish ways. Her heart softened. Yet, time and again, she'd witnessed his honorable, gentle side and, unlike many men of his station, he was taking responsibility for his illegitimate offspring, even if it *was* late in the game.

She was honestly surprised he hadn't fathered more than these two children. He had merely to walk into the room and her heart skipped a beat. He'd turned her insides molten hot when he'd waltzed her across the nursery room floor. Just the memory of his lips on her forehead sent butterflies skittering across the insides of her stomach.

She released a sigh. Why torture herself like this? The devil with that. She wanted him to kiss her, crush her to his chest, and… Her head whirled with thoughts of him gently laying her on his bed and coming down on top of her. Her heart beat fast. This had to end. He was her employer.

Charlotte tucked the covers more closely around Oliver before checking on Meg and Jane. She found them fast asleep. She straightened the nursery, then banked the fire for the night. When she was done, she dusted her hands and started toward her room, but stopped when the nursery door creaked open.

Her heart leapt. Alistair? Unable to stop the smile, she took a step toward the door. The smile died on her lips.

Captain Edwards, coatless and swaying on his feet, entered.

"*Sacre-bleu*," she swore. "Why are you here?"

"Why elshe?" he slurred the word.

"You're drunk," she said in disgust.

As he stumbled toward her, she retreated. "Leave, *now*." She pointed to the door.

"Leave? You *need* me."

"The devil I do. Get out."

He lurched forward and seized her by the waist.

"Get your hands off me!" Charlotte batted his chest.

He drove her backwards. Her back hit the wall. Pain lanced through her left shoulder blade. Fear spiked, but she forced a hard voice. "Don't be a fool."

"You want me," he whispered hoarsely. "You're my mistress, Charlotte. Come to bed."

"Your mistress?" He'd gone mad. "I am not your mistress."

His fingers dug into her shoulders. Charlotte twisted in an effort to break free. He grabbed her chin and forced her face upward, then mashed his mouth against hers. Bile rose. Tears threatened.

Think, she ordered herself. *Think*. Charlotte willed her muscles to relax and she started to fall. She ripped her mouth from his and drove her forehead into his nose. A sharp pain stabbed deep into her skull. The captain yowled and stumbled back, clutching his nose.

Charlotte's vision blurred. She glimpsed the poker leaning

against the hearth. Ignoring the pulsing pain in her head, she grabbed it and brandished it like a sword. "Leave, before I give you a solid drubbing."

"Losh, what's happening?" Meg's sleepy voice sounded from the door.

Captain Edwards staggered sideways, blood seeping between his fingers from his nose. He swung his gaze onto Meg, then spun and lurched out the door.

Charlotte dropped the poker, rushed to the door and shoved it closed. She stood with her weight against the wood and drew a long, shaky breath.

"Did the man threaten you, now?" Meg demanded.

Charlotte turned, but didn't leave the door. Meg stood in the doorway to her room, a shawl tossed over her nightdress and her big eyes filled with concern.

"No harm was done." Charlotte smoothed her dress to calm her nerves. "He was drunk. Most likely, he'll never remember the incident."

Meg's eyes narrowed. "We should tell his lordship. He'll boot the man straight out." She crossed to the hearth and picked up the skeleton key on the mantle, then went to the door. Charlotte stepped aside and she locked the door.

Meg straightened and handed her the key. "We should keep the door locked until the man is gone. Are you sure you're all right, Miss?"

Charlotte gave her a shaky smile. "I'm fine. You go to bed. We're perfectly safe now."

Meg hesitated, then nodded and bid her good night.

Charlotte glanced at the door. She'd been a victim of Captain Edwards' temper before. She'd thought him a mere pompous bully, but now... Fear rippled deep inside her, and even though she knew full well she'd locked the nursery door, she couldn't relax until she'd dragged a chair and propped it under the knob as well.

CHARLOTTE HAD JUST SAT THE CHILDREN AT THE BREAKFAST table when a sharp rap on the nursery door made her jump. Exchanging a quick glance with Meg, she strode to the door. More relief than she cared to admit flooded through her when she opened it to find Lady Cassilis's maid in the hallway.

"Good morning, Miss Atchenson." The young woman greeted her with a nervous smile. "Her ladyship requests your presence. At once."

Charlotte winced.

The maid's smile turned sympathetic.

"Och, I will watch the lad and lassie," Meg offered. "You'd best do as Lady Cassilis bids. 'Tis better for all of us when she's not kept waiting."

"Right then." Charlotte heaved a breath.

She darted to the mirror and quickly tucked in a few stray locks, then twirled, inspecting her new green muslin gown for anything out of order. This was the first dress Fanny had made for her. It would have been better not to accept the dress. But how did a governess refuse her employer's gift?

"She'll not find a thing to complain over, lass," Meg assured. "Unless it's the gown's too fine or you are late in arriving."

Charlotte snorted. "Most likely both," she said, and left with the maid.

Lady Cassilis thinned her lips upon Charlotte's arrival. Sitting at her secretary desk in a yellow morning dress, the woman clucked her tongue and shook her head in disapproval.

"You are such a pretentious servant." Her eyes raked Charlotte from head to toe. "Look at you, so finely dressed. Not one to know your place, are you?"

So, Meg had been right. Charlotte kept her eyes downcast, dipped into a respectful curtsey and murmured, "Good morning, my lady."

The woman humphed. "Fetch my rouge from the dye-shop. Be quick. I need it before Lady Ann arrives this afternoon." She turned away and began shuffling the papers on her secretary desk.

"Pardon?" Charlotte asked, confused.

Lady Cassilis glanced up, but her maid quickly stepped forward. "I'll be happy to explain it further to Miss Atchenson, my lady." She offered a curtsey of her own.

The woman nodded and turned back to her business.

Charlotte followed the maid out the door and back to the servants' stairs.

"I am afraid it's my fault she's asked you to do this." The young woman lifted the hem of her dress and revealed her bandaged left foot. "I twisted it on the stair last night. It's well enough for the castle, but not for a walk to the dye-shop in Maidens. Her ladyship could ask another, but..." the young woman smiled a bit ruefully.

"Her ladyship doesn't care for me," Charlotte finished with a dry laugh. "No matter. I am happy enough to help."

"It's not far," the young woman assured. "Maidens is straight down Piper's Brae, and it's a pleasant enough day for a walk."

"I'll just fetch my bonnet and coat." Charlotte smiled brightly, then hurried away.

"I will never understand the workings of her ladyship's mind," Meg tut-tutted in the nursery a few minutes later as Charlotte tied her bonnet. "What did you *do* to the woman? Why does she hate you so?"

Charlotte shrugged and they shared a laugh and, after seeing the children busy with their lessons, she hurried downstairs.

What had she done to antagonize Lady Cassilis? While the woman had detested her from the start, she'd apparently added another level of venom after Charlotte had caught her on the beach with that pockmarked man. Was the man a secret lover?

Charlotte snorted and rolled her eyes. What man would willingly embrace such a bitter prune?

Heavy mist shrouded the castle lawn as she hurried across the grass, still wet from the night's storm. She grimaced as cold water soaked through her thin boots. She hated wet feet.

As she neared the marshes and the Swan Pond, Alistair's mention of a man with a red-feathered, green hat sprang to mind. Now that she thought of it, Oliver had worn such a hat in the stables. It was a rather odd style of hat. She wouldn't have thought it popular enough for two of them to be seen around the castle. She'd have to ask Oliver where he'd come by the thing and where it now was. Lord Cassilis would want to know about the hat. It was too—

She started at a thundering of hooves behind her. She turned. In the mist, she discerned a rider galloping her way. As he approached, she hurried to the side of the road. Before she realized his intent, he veered her way, swooped down, and hauled her across his lap.

It had to be Captain Edwards.

"Devil take you!" She pummeled his chest with her fists. "Unhand me, you fool—

"There, there, lass," rumbled a familiar deep voice. "Och, you're even smaller than you look."

Charlotte froze, torn between shock, relief—and anger. "*Damnation!* Have you lost your mind?" she demanded. "What gentleman snatches a lady off the street? I thought you—" She broke off.

Alistair chuckled and let the horse canter a few paces more before slowing the animal to a walk. His strong thighs shifted beneath her as he twisted her around, so she sat sideways across his lap.

He'd forgone the coat, vest, and cravat in favor of a loose, white, puff-sleeved shirt with a large green Cassilis plaid thrown over his broad shoulders.

He caught her chin with his thumb and tilted her head back toward his. "Where did such a wee thing like you learn to swear like a sailor?"

She squirmed, embarrassed. "It's a detestable habit. My great-uncle was a navy man. He raised me as his own after my mother died. But I offer it as no excuse—"

Alistair chuckled. "I need no apology, lass. Far from it. I confess, I find you a damn sight more interesting than the ladies at Culzean, nattering behind their fans."

The compliment made her heart skip a beat. "You would dash their hopes if they heard you say that, my lord."

"Hopes?" His lips curved into a smile above his dimpled chin. "I've given them no such thing. Truth be told, I can't tell you how many guests I even have—or half of their names."

They shared a laugh.

His arm flexed about her waist and his expression grew serious. "Why are you walking alone?"

Charlotte shifted uneasily, too aware of the firm, muscular thighs beneath her bottom and the hardness of his chest pressed against her shoulder. Biting her lip in an effort to clear her thoughts, she replied, "Lady Cassilis sent me on an errand, my lord. She is in need of her rouge before luncheon is served."

He brought his horse to a stop and stared down at her. His eyes darkened. "My name is Alistair," he whispered. "Say it."

Her stomach flipped and she managed a whispered, "I can scarcely call you that, my lord."

His thick lashes lowered. "Why not? A lass who raps my knuckles with a spoon shouldn't balk at addressing me by my given name."

She blurted, "You *were* misbehaving."

"Was I?" he teased.

The seductive timber of his voice made her shiver. It was time to direct the conversation to safer territory. Biting her bottom lip yet again, she began, "It is my duty—"

"If you bite your lip one more time, Charlotte, I will not be held accountable for my actions," he warned.

She started, unable to look away from the raw hunger in his eyes. Her breath quickened as his arm tightened around her waist.

Neither moved.

A gull cawed in the skies overhead. The wind rustled through the trees, bringing with it the rich scent of damp earth and wet leaves.

The pounding of horses' hooves on the moist ground broke into the moment.

The realization that the horsemen were already upon them struck them both at the same time, and they turned their heads in unison to face the newcomers.

Nicholas arrived in a jingle of bits and creaking leather, three other riders in tow. The distinct twinkle in his blue eyes announced he'd just witnessed their near kiss and seen it for exactly what it was.

"A good day to you." He grinned. "We're out for a bit of hawking, my dear fellow. Care to join us?"

"Not at all," Alistair answered mildly. "Please, as you were." He backed his horse off the road and waved them on with an impatient hand.

Nicholas laughed, nodded farewell with an even wider grin, and trotted his horse down the road, his companions falling in line behind him. As the last horseman passed, Charlotte stiffened.

Damnation. There he was again. Captain Edwards—with angry eyes and—she stifled a laugh—and a large, purple bruise on his nose. He shot her a glare and her amusement vanished. For one long, horrible moment, she feared he would stop and confront her. Instead, he stuck out his jaw and rode on.

Once out of earshot, Alistair remarked, "Captain Edwards seems quite taken with you."

She snorted. "Hardly." Perhaps she *should* let him know of the Captain's advances last night. The man certainly deserved the consequences.

"Do you not find him an honorable, tall, strapping fellow? Rather fetching?" Alistair asked.

"Honorable?" she blurted. "He is a despicable man." Realizing her mistake, she hurried to add, "Forgive me, my lord, I should not speak of your guest in that manner."

He threw his head back and gave a deep laugh. When his eyes met hers once again, they were filled with obvious relief. "Please, I beg you, speak more ill of the man. It brightens my mood."

She blinked, then found herself mirroring his smile. "Then…you do not care for him?"

"I cannot bear the pompous fool," he admitted. "He's a chaperone to Lady Brexley, nothing more."

The pompous fool. Her mood shifted and she glanced away. She had to tell the truth. "I was once engaged to him." She kept her eyes directed at her lap. "Indeed, he is pompous beyond belief."

"Were you madly in love?" he asked in a quiet voice.

She snapped her head up. "Devil take the man, but *no.* My father owed him a great deal of money. Truth be told, I was payment—and at sixteen years of age, I knew of nothing but how to agree." She hesitated. "The scandalous circumstances surrounding my father's death inspired the Captain to seek his freedom—for which I will ever be grateful. The man cares more for his reputation than anything else."

"Ah, yes, the ten shillings." Alistair snorted under his breath.

It took a moment for the words to sink in. She frowned, astonished. "How would you know that?"

His green eyes twinkled. "I heard this tale from your very own lips, Charlotte." His grin went lopsided. "That first night, when the highland whisky loosened your tongue."

Her cheeks warmed.

He cocked a brow. "We had best be off to Maidens for Lady Cassilis's rouge. We will make a quick ride of it. It's not far."

He kicked his horse's flank, and the animal broke into a trot. Charlotte threw her arms around Alistair's neck. He laughed and urged the horse on as she buried her face against his shoulder and held on for dear life.

Ten minutes later, Alistair slowed the horse to a walk and Charlotte surveyed the small fishing village of Maidens perched on the shores of the Firth of Clyde. Gulls circled overhead as Alistair clattered down the cobbled lane, past the market cross to the dye-shop just off the main square.

He halted before a small, stone building, then dismounted and lifted her down from the saddle. Placing her lightly on her feet, he kept his strong hands around her waist until she looked up. He really did have the most unusual eyes, bright green, flecked with gray and blue and ringed with thick, dark lashes.

"My lord." A male voice intruded upon the moment. "A good day to you."

A small smile played over his lips as Alistair stepped back and Charlotte faced an old man with snow-white hair standing in the door of his shop.

"A right good day to you, Sean," Alistair replied.

"I've a message for Nicholas," the old man said. "If you'd be so kind as to tell him. He asked me to keep an eye out for strange happenings in Maidens, no matter how small."

Alistair lifted an inquisitive brow. "What have you found?"

"It's Thomas, my lord, Thomas Graves. You'd recall him, I'd think."

Alistair knit his brows in thought. "Thomas? The same Thomas Graves who worked my father's estate as a footman when I was a wee lad?"

"Aye." The old man nodded. "One and the same, my lord,

though he's always been a worthless fellow, a rabble rouser, drifting from fight to fight." He shook his head in disgust.

"So, what has this Thomas to do with Nicholas?" Alistair prodded.

"He's struck it rich," the shopkeeper answered. "A man who's not done a day's honest work in years. 'Tis odd. How he came into money is a mystery, but 'twill be no mystery in how he loses it, with all the drink he's after."

Alistair's dark eyes turned speculative. "Where might Thomas be now?"

"The man rides off north every morning, but returns to Maidens drunk afore the sun sets."

Alistair nodded his thanks and turned back to Charlotte. He held out his hand and told the man, "We've come for Lady Cassilis's rouge."

"Ah, then step inside, step inside." The shopkeeper waved for them to follow as he disappeared into his shop.

The pleasant scent of wet wool and dried lavender greeted Charlotte as she stepped over the dye-shop's threshold. A long worktable ran down the center of the room, holding a collection of black iron pots and wooden tubs filled with crushed leaves and water. Discarded stems littered the floor and skeins of wool hung from the rafters, intermixed with bundles of dried flowers, leaves, and herbs. A large set of wooden shelves lined one wall, filled with rows of tiny clay pots.

Near the back of the shop stood a small table stacked with books, and one book in particular drew Charlotte—a leather-bound cookery book, like her mother's. She picked the book off the shelf and slowly ran her fingers over the cover, then leafed through a few pages. Emotion choked her.

"That's fine workmanship there, lass," the shopkeeper said as he shuffled through a mound of paper-wrapped packages on his worktable.

Charlotte looked up and smiled. "My mother had one like

this." She blinked back tears and turned. Alistair watched from his position near the door. She averted her eyes. Strange. She hadn't wept over her mother in years. She had no wish to do so now in front of onlookers.

"Lady Cassilis's rouge." The shopkeeper picked up a small package from the counter on the left wall and offered it to Charlotte.

Accepting it with a quick dip of thanks, she crossed the room and stepped out into the street as Alistair and the old man spoke.

The scattered clouds had vanished entirely, leaving the sky a rich, bright blue. Birds twittered from nearby trees. A dog barked in the distance. She closed her eyes, enjoying the warmth of the sunlight on her face and the distant lull of waves breaking on the rocky shore.

At the sound of a boot scraping wood behind her, Charlotte glanced up as Alistair stepped from the store, a solemn smile on his lips.

"Shall we?" He nodded toward his horse.

The thought of sitting across his had thighs the entire way back both unnerved *and* excited her, but the notion was unwise. "I have been enough trouble, my lord—"

He closed the argument by plucking the rouge from her grasp.

The return journey was far more intimate. Alistair's hand rested on her hip. He walked the horse at a slow pace. She hid a smile. He behaved like a green lad with a pretty girl. But he was no green lad. He felt so large and warm around her. She found it difficult to think of anything other than his thighs flexing beneath her buttocks and the warm chest she leaned her shoulder against.

"Join me at dinner tonight," he said suddenly.

She snapped her head up. "Dinner?" she repeated.

He shrugged. "Why no'? Culzean is my home and a

governess at the dinner table is common enough."

An image flitted across her mind of shocked dinner guests, when they heard her flavorful brand of French. A snort of laughter escaped her lips before she quickly cleared her throat, and said, "Not I, my lord. I fear you would regret it."

He lifted a brow. "Why? Are your manners uncouth? How do you eat? Do you snuffle the soup?" The corners of his mouth curved upwards. "I confess, now I am curious."

"My lord, I may very well astonish you by drinking the rose water from the fingerbowls. Trust me, your reputation is the better for not knowing."

He gave a hearty chuckle, in which she joined, but then his gaze dropped to linger on her lips.

"What of the ball?" The amusement had faded from his voice. "It will be thrown in my honor at the end of the month. Surely, you cannot refuse to attend?" He shifted beneath her and his hand slid lower on her hip.

Charlotte swallowed. It was dangerous to be so close to the man. "Surely, my lord, you wouldn't chance such a thing. I fear I dance like a—"

His dark lashes lowered and he shushed her with a finger on her lips. His finger lingered a heartbeat, then slid down over her bottom lip.

"I have danced with you already, have I not?" he asked in a thick voice. "You were a feather in my arms, Charlotte."

Her heart thudded wildly.

Alistair suddenly pulled rein. He hugged her close, then swung his long leg over the pommel and slid from the saddle. They touched the ground and he lowered her feet until she stood. He stared a moment then pressed his palm into the small of her back, locking her into place against him. Charlotte shivered at the hunger in his eyes. She was lost. She knew it. She couldn't resist the man. He placed a finger beneath her chin and brushed the line of her jaw with his thumb.

He bent down and whispered over her lips, "I want to kiss you, Charlotte."

"Please," she whispered back. *Please.*

He smiled. She closed her eyes, at first feeling awkward, but forgot everything with the first light brush of his mouth against hers. He pressed several soft kisses on her mouth, tasting her longer each time, while his thumb stroked her cheek.

"So sweet," he murmured against her mouth, then his tongue traced the seam of her lips.

Her mind whirled when his fingers slid along the sensitive flesh of her neck, then cupped her nape. He flicked her bottom lip, softly at first but with an increasing, yet gentle intensity that coaxed her mouth open. She shivered at the press of her breasts against his chest.

His tongue skimmed the inner surface of her bottom lip, then ventured deeper. She tensed, caught off guard. Captain Edwards had kissed her before, but never like this. The man had smashed his lips against hers and she'd been only relieved when he stopped. But this? She shuddered, savoring each brush of Alistair's tongue dancing over hers.

She melted against him. He tightened his hold and plundered her mouth. Shiver after delicious shiver slid down her spine. Tentatively, she pushed the tip of her tongue between his lips to taste him. He moaned, his fingers sliding up her neck and tangled in her hair as his mouth devoured hers. His hand slid from the base of her spine up the line of her back and pressed her hard into him. The ridges of his chest pressed her breasts.

He tore his lips away abruptly. "Smoke," he said in a hoarse whisper. He glanced over his shoulder.

The next instant, her nostrils stung with the smell of smoke. Alistair dashed to his grazing horse and vaulted into the saddle as Charlotte scanned the sky.

"There." She pointed to a plum of smoke visible through a break in the trees ahead.

"It's the old icehouse," he said. "Come, Charlotte."

She lunged toward him and Alistair stretched out a hand. She grabbed his arm and he swung her up into the saddle behind him.

"Hold tight," he ordered.

She threw her arms about his waist and pressed her cheek to his back an instant before he kicked the horse into a mad gallop. The horse leapt forward, running so fast that the trees flew by in a blur. They went no more than a quarter mile before Alistair turned the animal from the road. The horse sailed over a low hedge and raced through the underbrush.

As they neared the fire, smoke hung heavy in the air. Alistair drew rein near what appeared to be a door carved into the side the stone hill. A column of black smoke funneled through the opening.

"Nae! Please!" cried a faint voice.

Charlotte froze. "Oliver!" she gasped in horror. "He's inside. But how—"

Alistair leapt from the saddle, then raced to the door. Charlotte slid from the saddle. Her heart nearly stopped. There was too much smoke. He would never make it out. Oliver—A sob clogged her throat. Alistair reached the door. Flames licked the doorway. Alistair yanked his arm up to shield his face.

Fear nearly buckled her legs. The flames, he was so close to the flame. Tears streamed down her face. She stumbled toward him. Alistair whipped off his coat and swung it over his head. Her heart thundered. Charlotte spotted movement in the trees near the door. It couldn't be. She veered toward the trees.

Oliver lunged from within the trees. "Nae!" he shouted, and raced toward Alistair.

Charlotte whipped in the direction of Alistair. "Stop!" she shouted.

He ducked his head in readiness to dash into the smoke.

"Alistair!" she shouted as loud as she could.

He twisted and looked at her. She pointed to his right. He turned in that direction—then flung his coat aside and shot toward Oliver.

Alistair reached Oliver and swung the boy up into her arms, then crashed to his knees, Oliver sobbing. Charlotte reached them and cried out at sight of a smoldering spot on the upper sleeve of Alistair's shirt. She dropped to her knees beside them and slapped at the cloth until it no longer smoked. A raw, red burn marred the muscled flesh on his upper arm.

"You will live," she told him in a matter-of-fact voice, despite the thudding of her heart. "Painful, to be sure, but not life-threatening. Thank heavens." She suddenly felt weak, and plopped down onto her backside beside them.

A crash sounded inside the cavern. Charlotte cried out and yanked her gaze on the open doorway.

The fire cannot hurt us," Alistair said. "It will burn out inside the cavern."

To her surprise, flames no longer tried to escape. Alistair held Oliver close as the boy clung to him as if he would never let go.

Finally, Alistair stirred. "What happened, lad?" he asked.

Oliver buried his face in Alistair's shoulder and sobbed, "Why does my father hate me?"

Alistair frowned. "Hate you? I do not—"

"Not you," Oliver lifted his head, his tears leaving trails on his soot-covered cheeks. "My father. Charles."

Alistair closed his eyes.

Charlotte frowned.

"I know who you are," Oliver whispered. "You are my uncle."

Charlotte stared.

Uncle?

CHAPTER 11

You're my uncle.

Alistair sighed. So, the lad knew the truth. "Who told you I wasn't your father?" he asked softly. "How long have you known?"

Oliver's lips trembled and tears streaked his grimy cheeks. "My mum. She always told me my da's name was Charles. When she..." He blanched. "He left us at Lady Prescott's door, told us you'd come and that you were a good man, unlike himself. Said you'd see us raised good and proper..." The sobs racked his thin shoulders.

Alistair gathered him closer. So, the boy had known from the start. It explained the sullen challenges and the refusal to participate. It even answered why he'd crept into Charles's bedchamber. What of Charles? At least he'd seen his children to Lady Prescott's door before running off who-knew-where.

"It's no matter, lad." Alistair patted his nephew's shoulder. "Fathers are the men who rear you." It had been that way for him, anyway, with Foster.

Oliver wiggled out of his grasp. "Why didn't you deny us?" he asked.

He met the boy's gaze steadily. "I know how dangerous it is to live without roots. I may not have fathered you, Oliver, but I'll be a father to you now. I swear it."

To his surprise, the lad vehemently shook his head. "Father," he spat, looking angry at the mere word. "Nae. I would rather call you Uncle."

"Aye, then." Alistair clamped his hand on the lad's shoulder. "It does no' matter what name I am called. You are home. Where you belong. You're a Cassilis, of my own blood, and a member of the clan, and that's all there's to say on the matter."

At the thud of approaching hooves, they looked up as men emerged from the trees. Another loud crash sounded inside the ice house.

"Damnation," Alistair cursed. More smoke billowed from the icehouse door. More brandy kegs must have caught fire.

Alistair released Oliver and rose. "There's little worth saving, lads," he informed the men.

After completion of the new icehouse the previous year, he'd used the old one to store empty brandy kegs and wine barrels. There was nothing left of them now. And since the icehouse was made of stone, once the fire died, there would be no real harm. He didn't believe the fire could jump from within the cavern, but Alistair instructed his men to stand guard until they were certain the fire had died. He then returned his attention to Oliver, who now stood alongside Charlotte. The lad pulled a felt green hat with a broken red feather from inside his shirt.

"I came here to fetch you this, sir." He extended the hat toward him. "You said you wanted the man."

Alistair accepted the hat. "You have seen this man before?"

Oliver nodded earnestly. "He comes here often."

Alistair turned the hat over in his hands. Strange. "Do you know his name? Where he's from?"

The boy shook his head.

"How did the fire start?" Alistair probed.

Oliver dropped his gaze. So, this question made him uncomfortable.

"You were inside the icehouse, I take it?"

Oliver nodded and Alistair's chest tightened. If the boy had been trapped inside… He shook off the thought. You could have been harmed," Alistair said in a stern voice. "You are to stay in the castle proper and not wander about the estate. If you have a matter of concern, you will speak with me first before taking matters into your own hands. Do you understand?"

Oliver nodded.

"Come, let's return to the castle," Alistair said.

Charlotte looked pale, and he read the remnants of fear in her eyes. A sudden gust of wind tugged at her loose, errant curls. He wanted to hold her close, tell her all would be well, but he could do nothing now but wait.

Her eyes dropped to his arm. "You're injured. You need treatment, my lord."

He hardly noticed the pain. He enjoyed the softness in her eyes so much more. "After a bit of ointment, all will be well," he said.

After retrieving his horse, they set off for Culzean again, a somewhat bedraggled party covered in grime and walking in silence. Alistair carried the hat. Who was the man, and what was he doing in the ice house? Alistair glance at Oliver. How had the boy known the hat was there to begin with?

The pain of Alistair's burn grew with each step, but for a time, he distracted himself tolerably well with Charlotte's slender, winsome form and the memory of her kiss. Her lips had tasted so sweet, so pure. He could only think of devouring them again—and more besides.

They reached the castle and were greeted by Foster and a mix of worried servants and guests. A doctor was summoned.

Alistair found himself swept up the stairs. On the second floor, he came face-to-face with Lady Cassilis.

She'd heard news of the fire. "A fire? In the icehouse? How is that possible?" Her gaze fell to the green hat he still clutched and she paled.

Alistair's thoughts snapped to attention. The woman had clearly seen the hat before. He folded it over in his hands.

She noticeably flinched, then, head held high, she sailed down the corridor toward her apartments.

He arched a brow. Perhaps, he merely had to find the owner of the hat to discover how Lady Cassilis planned to wrest Culzean from his grip.

"Your arm, my lord," Charlotte's soft voice sounded by his side.

Alistair looked down to see her still standing there, holding Oliver's hand. A frown marred her brow.

He smiled gently. Those lips. How he wanted to kiss them. "I'll tend to it now, lass," he promised. As an afterthought, he added, "Do not forget, Miss Atchenson, I fully expect you to join me at the dinner table this evening."

Her eyes widened and she opened her mouth to protest.

But he cut her off with the whispered words, "If you're not there, I'll fetch you down myself."

THE DINNER HOUR FOUND ALISTAIR WITH HIS ARM TREATED AND properly bandaged. With the icehouse fire doused and with no real harm done, he'd settled in his study with Nicholas to ponder the recent events.

"Odd." Nicholas tapped his long finger on his glass of whisky. "How could the lad set such a blaze?"

"He clearly didn't set the blaze." Alistair nodded at the hat. "The hat's owner must have." Again, Lady Cassilis's reaction played in his mind. What was her relationship with the man? He rubbed his bottom lip in thought.

"I'll ride out to Maidens in the morning. Maybe folk there have seen the hat and can shed some light on the matter," Nicholas offered. "I'll see what this Thomas has to say about his newfound wealth, as well. No doubt, if I buy him a drink, he'll sing like a songbird."

"No doubt, indeed," Alistair agreed.

The dinner gong sounded.

Alistair thought of Charlotte and smiled. He would wager she had found some excuse to avoid dinner—not that he'd let her.

"You're in love with her." Nicholas' soft voice intruded on his thoughts. "I can always tell when you're thinking of her. Your smile betrays you."

Alistair shrugged. Why deny it?

As the mournful strains of the pipes filled the air, they left the study and went to the dining room, each lost in their own thoughts. Alistair entered first and took in the fine dinner table set with a silver candelabra, an epergne resplendent with artificial flowers, and rare bottles of Rhenish wine, but no Charlotte.

"I fear your fair bird has flown," Nicholas murmured at his elbow.

Alistair caught sight of his stepmother entering the room, and snorted, "No doubt, she's been chased off by the vulture."

Nicholas grinned.

As if sensing herself the subject of their conversation, Lady Cassilis called across the room, "Come, Alistair. Let dinner begin."

Alistair paused. Sitting through course after course of casseroles, roasts, truffles, puddings, and Italian creams was bad enough. Add the ladies embellishing the same scandals over and over, and the thought of dinner was downright unbearable.

He strode toward the door and caught sight of Captain Edwards standing in a corner with a flower in his button hole and a container of snuff on his palm. Alistair shook his head. He would have to have a talk with Nicholas about his taste in friends.

Seeing the man only made Alistair hasten toward the exit.

"Alistair!" Lady Cassilis called. "Pray tell, *where* are you going?"

He paused and, unable to resist, answered, "I grow weary of hearing the same scandals, Lady Cassilis. I choose to create new ones."

Nicholas burst into hearty laughter amidst gasps of shock— and Alistair strode out the door, headed to the grand staircase.

He took the steps two at a time. On the top floor, he found the object of his attention strolling the candle-lit corridor, her attention buried in the pages of a book while she balanced a tray on her hip.

He had her now. Alistair crept up behind her. Once within reach, he plucked the tray from her grasp. She whirled as he set it on a nearby marble-topped table.

Sir!" she cried.

He caught her about the waist and whirled her around, then pushed her back against the wall.

"My lord." Her eyes widened with surprise as she hugged the book close to her breast.

Alistair braced his hands against the wall on each side of her head and smiled down at her. "Alistair," he corrected. "Were you not to join me for dinner?"

Her lashes fluttered and she tilted her head toward the tray. "Oliver needed a milk posset—"

"Excuses." He inhaled deep of the heady perfume of her hair and leaned closer for a kiss.

She ducked under his arm and retreated two paces.

He pushed from the wall and arched a brow.

She lifted her chin.

He grinned. No matter. He had a few tricks of his own. He knew the value of patience.

"Surely, you should attend your guests," she said. The devilish gleam he had come to love returned to her lively hazel eyes. "You will disappoint the ladies. They will miss out on your carving of the beef, my lord."

"Alistair," he corrected. He crossed his arms over his chest and leaned a shoulder against the wall. He frowned. "The carving of the beef? Is the carving of meat a manly thing admired by women?"

"To be sure." She gave a solemn nod completely at odds with the teasing spark in her eyes. "Does it not prove you've been trained in good fashion? A graceful performance is presumed to mark a person—or so it says here in *The Fine Art of Deportment* which ensures it must be true." She lifted the book she grasped.

With a dry chuckle, Alistair plucked it from her hand. He glanced at the title, then tossed it on the table next to the tray. "I see, Miss Atchenson. You would rather read about such things than attend a dinner where I might impress you with a wondrous demonstration?"

She laughed, her eyes crinkling at the corners. "I fear I would not be properly impressed, my lord. At least, not until I have finished the book to learn just what exactly *should* impress me. I confess, until a moment ago, I never thought the carving of meat to be an art."

He studied her. "Tell me, what does impress you?"

"I fear I am not a proper enough lady to know—"

Quick as a flash, he yanked her into his arms. She squeaked. There was no book between them now. Her soft breasts pressed against his chest. Her eyes were large, wide, and soft.

"You swear like a sailor," he murmured. How long would he be able to resist her? His body needed her touch. "And you're unimpressed with manly knife skills at the dinner table, yet..." He allowed his voice to trail away as the alluring depths of her hazel eyes drew him in. "If you keep looking at me like that, Charlotte, I will have to kiss you," he warned in a hoarse whisper. "Propriety be damned."

This time, she didn't slip away. He covered her mouth with his. She melted beneath him as his tongue demanded immediate entry. She opened at once. He delved inside her hot, sweet mouth and sparred with her tongue.

He pressed her against the wall as their tongues danced, entwined, and tasted one another. She felt so delicate in his arms. She responded to his every touch, each nip of his teeth. Alistair twirled one of her errant curls around his finger, as he began to feather a slow line of kisses along her jaw and nibbled the sensitive skin beneath her earlobe. She shuddered.

"There she is," he breathed in her ear.

"She?" Charlotte panted.

He drew back enough to see her face "The minx I have glimpsed here and there." He dropped another kiss on her mouth and grazed her bottom lip with his teeth. "Do let her out to play more often, sweetheart."

"Perhaps she should be tamed," she suggested in velvet tones.

He snorted and raked his gaze down her body. "Tamed? Never. Never with me. I say let her run loose and as free as the wind. She's welcome to rap my knuckles with a spoon and drink the rose water each day of the week."

A glimmer of humor arced through her eyes and her long lashes fluttered.

He growled. He needed more of her. Nothing else mattered. He drew two fingertips lightly over her lips. "You're so bonny, lass," he said before he reclaimed her mouth in a hot, urgent kiss. He threaded his fingers into her hair, and tugged out the pins to free the curly tresses. She leaned into him. He deepened the kiss. Hot need demanded he possess her. He slid his hands lower down her spine.

Charlotte tore free. "Damnation." She bit her bottom lip in a gesture that drove him mad. "I have no will when it comes to you."

"How can I object to that?" He caught her bottom lip between his teeth and nibbled. She stilled, but he glimpsed the rise and fall of her breasts. His blood heated. He forced himself to break away. "I am not a dishonorable man, though you tempt me to the very hair's breadth of it, I must confess." Her gaze locked with his. "I am not my brother, Charlotte. I will enjoy your lips, aye, but my intentions are honorable."

Her eyes widened in shock. "Impossible."

That made him chuckle. "Oh? You find it easier to accept me as your lover?"

She blushed. "Heavens, but…no…I…it…" Taking a deep breath, she lifted her chin and went back to simply, "Impossible."

"Tell me, truthfully, Charlotte. Would you hesitate to accept me were I a stable hand, a sailor, or a cartwright?"

"If only you *were*." She sighed. "For then I could not refuse you."

Alistair threw back his head and laughed. She frowned and he couldn't resist nuzzling her ear again. "Then it is done, lass. For I have been all three, a stable hand, a sailor, *and* a cartwright. You cannot refuse me now, aye?"

She stared. Then she shook her head and laughed. Once again, he was lost. Alistair crushed her against him like a man possessed. He groaned against her mouth, and when she wrapped her arms around his neck and her tongue began an exploration of her own, he nearly came undone.

He pressed hot, open-mouthed kisses to her collarbone, but

it was a mistake, the passion it unleashed almost carried him too far. He tore himself from her and rested his forehead against hers.

He drew a long, ragged breath. "You have an uncommon way of heating my blood, lass."

She looked up, her eyes glittering in the candlelight.

"Go, Charlotte," he warned. He was moments away from sweeping her into his arms and carrying her to his bed. "Or else I will make myself a liar."

She hesitated and hope surged that she might insist he take her to his bed. Then she slipped out of his arms. He watched her walk at a sedate pace until she rounded the corner up ahead.

CHAPTER 12

CHARLOTTE NEARED THE NURSERY. SHE COVERED HER CHEEKS with her hands. How could she have acted with such abandon? Gooseflesh raced across her arms with the memory of his warm breath on her skin.

Make himself a liar? If only he *would.*

The hungry look in his green eyes had underscored the meaning of those words. She'd have let him take her to bed, right willingly. Charlotte paused before the nursery door and took a deep breath to compose herself. Whatever beast she'd unleashed within her heart certainly wasn't going to allow itself to become caged again—for better or worse.

When her breathing slowed, she opened the nursery door and entered.

Meg sat in front of the fire mending Jane's petticoat and looked up in alarm. "Losh, what happened?" she asked, but then relaxed and chuckled. "Ah, I see. You have been with his lordship, aye?"

Charlotte blinked. "What do you mean?"

"Your lips." She chortled. "They call those kiss-swollen lips. Hie yourself to the mirror and have a wee look.

She didn't go to the mirror. She didn't dare. Covering her cheeks with her palms, she moaned, "I do think I can do this, Meg."

"Think?" Meg rose and stretched. "It's simple enough, lass. All you have to do is answer one wee question."

Charlotte drew a long breath. "What question is that?"

With a twinkle in her eye, the redheaded maid said in a conspiratorial whisper, "It's 'do you *want* to'?"

Did she *want* to? Damnation, that's all she *wanted* to do.

Heat crept up her cheeks.

Meg grinned, and Charlotte knew her cheeks were flaming.

CHARLOTTE YAWNED AND INDULGED IN A LONG, LUXURIOUS stretch in the sun that streamed through the window. She hadn't felt so relaxed in months. She sat up and glanced out the window, into a bright, sunny day. It took a moment to note the angle of the sun, far higher than usual. *Sacre-bleu!* It was midday. She bolted out of bed, threw on her dress, then fled into the nursery, still gathering her wayward curls into a knot.

Meg and the children, seated at the table, glanced up at her in surprise.

"I fear I have overslept," she confessed.

"Och, no worries, lass." Meg's freckled face melted into laughter as she waved the children back to their studies. "His lordship came earlier, but when I told him you still slept, he ordered you not be disturbed." Meg drew herself up to her full height and planted her hands on her wide hips as she spoke in a low voice that imitated his lordship, "Let the lass sleep as long as she pleases, Meg. I shall come for her later."

Charlotte groaned.

A sly look crossed Meg's face. She stepped close and playfully dug her elbow into Charlotte's ribs. "Methinks I should start calling you 'her ladyship', aye?"

"Heavens, no," she quickly shushed the jolly maid.

Meg merely laughed and hurried to the hearth. She scooped up a letter from the mantle and came back to Charlotte. "Has his lordship's seal." She dropped it into Charlotte's hand with a knowing wink, then returned to her chair.

Charlotte stared at the letter. What could Alistair possibly have to say to her in a letter? She escaped to her room, broke the red wax seal, and read:

Come to the stables. At once.

Alistair

The letter's curt, cold words sounded unlike the man, but perhaps he'd been in a hurry…or worse, perhaps something was wrong. It didn't matter. Her heart began to race at the thought of seeing him again. After she buttoned herself into a newly-made, light blue pelisse, she informed Meg and the children she would return as soon as she could and hurried from the nursery.

Minutes later, Charlotte slipped from the castle. Wind whipped her skirts as she crossed the lawn, toward the clock tower and the stables beyond. *He wanted to see her.* Concern flooded her. Should she brace herself against disappointment? Perhaps, he had called her to the stables to apologize for the kiss?

Her step faltered. "Really, Charlotte," she admonished. "He is an earl. You are a governess. This cannot end well."

But the memory of his gentle lips on hers swept all thoughts away. What had she to fear? Never had she met so honorable a man. He'd shown nothing but honor from the start. How many men would accept social disgrace in order to spare their nephew pain? During those moments at the ice house, she'd never found a man more handsome in her entire life. She quickened her pace and arrived at the stables to find men pitching soiled hay into a cart.

"Good day, Miss." One raised his hand to his hat. "How can I help you?"

Dipping her head in greeting, she smiled and replied, "His lordship bade me join him here, sir."

The man drew his brows together. "His lordship's already done with his morning ride. He is back up to the castle."

Of course. She'd overslept. Charlotte thanked the man, then hurried back the way she'd come. Might she return to the nursery to find him there? She entered the castle, wondering what next to do, when she met Foster in the hallway and showed the old piper the letter.

"His lordship is in his study," he said. "Come with me, Miss." He led her down the hallway.

Alistair's study came into view up ahead. The door stood open.

"So, the owner of the hat is Thomas?" Nicholas' voice drifted to them. "And the source of his newfound wealth is Lady Cassilis. Why would Lady Cassilis pay the town drunk?"

"Something happened in that icehouse, yesterday." Charlotte recognized Alistair's deep tone. "We now know that Thomas was there, and Lady Cassilis could not hide her interest in the place when she spoke with me. She must have been there as well. Perhaps the lad stumbled across—"

Charlotte and Foster reached the room and she looked through the open doorway. Alistair lounged in a brown, wingback chair with one booted foot propped on a small side table. He radiated such lazy grace and primal heat that butterflies danced in her stomach. He wore a white linen shirt, and the gray trousers hugging his long, muscular legs were outright indecent.

As the piper motioned her forward, Charlotte entered. Alistair's gaze met hers. He jumped to his feet and crossed the room in three long strides. Her fears faded at once.

"Charlotte," he murmured. "What a pleasure to see you. What brings you here? Surely, Oliver hasn't gotten into mischief yet again?" He smiled.

"Oliver is studying, my lord." She smiled back and extended the letter toward him. "I…came because of this."

He took the note and threaded his warm fingers through hers. She allowed him to tug her to the chair he'd vacated by the fire, keenly aware of Nicholas' curious gaze.

"What letter is this?" Alistair turned the letter over as she sat down on the chair.

That surprised her. "Meg said you left it for me."

Alistair frowned. Quickly, he flipped it open and scanned the contents. His brows inched up in surprise. "I did no' write this."

Nicholas plucked the letter from his hand and read it. "The mysteries in this house multiply by the day." He turned his ice-blue eyes on her. "When did Meg receive this?"

"I assumed this morning, but I cannot be certain."

"Odd," Alistair murmured.

"Allow me to speak with Meg," Nicholas offered. With a curt nod, he strode to the door and vanished into the corridor.

Uneasy, Charlotte stood. "I shall not interrupt you, my—"

"Alistair," he interjected. "My Alistair. I like that." His expression clouded as he reached down and absently twisted one of her wayward curls around his finger. "This letter alarms me."

"Who would write such a thing?" She frowned.

He cupped her cheek with his palm. "We will find out." He gave her shoulder a reassuring squeeze. "Sit," he gently ordered.

She obeyed and he strode to the fireplace.

Silence fell.

Charlotte remained in the chair with folded hands as he

added wood to the fire. The flames crackled in a mesmerizing dance of light, drawing Charlotte's thoughts far away, until it seemed only a moment later before the baronet returned.

Nicholas held the letter up between two fingers. "We have a mystery. Meg found this last night on the table in the nursery. She meant to give it to Miss Atchenson but, as Miss Atchenson returned late…" A small smile hovered over his lips.

Concern flashed across Alistair's face. "Who would draw Charlotte out to the stables at night, and for what purpose?"

"Something smells foul," Nicholas agreed.

Alistair turned to Charlotte. "Have you an enemy here?"

An enemy? She shook her head, even as her thoughts went to Lady Cassilis. The woman had been angry over the accidental meeting on the beach. She wondered if she should mention it.

"I shall look into the matter." Alistair took the letter from Nicholas. "Surely, someone must have seen who delivered this."

Charlotte rose. "Then I shall return to the children, my lord."

He caught her smoothly by the arm and pulled her close. She tensed when he planted a kiss on the top of her head, then melted when he said, "Stay close to the castle and do not walk alone until I get to the bottom of this."

"I will," she promised. Keenly aware of Nicholas watching, she took her leave.

Charlotte hurried down the corridor. She'd just placed her foot on the bottom stair of the servants' stairs when a familiar, and unwelcome, voice spoke behind her.

"Charlotte."

Captain Edwards stepped up beside her. Wearing a dark blue, squared-cut tailcoat, he held his hat in his hands as his fingers fiddled with the brim.

"May I have a word with you, Charlotte?" he asked in a quiet voice.

She narrowed her eyes. "Why?"

He hesitated, then drew a long breath through his nostrils. "I…owe you an apology."

Her mouth dropped open. Never had she expected to hear the man utter those words.

A maid passed them and hurried up the stairs. He waited until she'd vanished before continuing, "Please, Charlotte. I am leaving soon. I wish…to part on friendlier terms. I have much…to seek forgiveness for. I beg you, spare a few moments."

Again, another maid appeared, this one carrying an armful of linens. Charlotte stepped aside, allowing her to pass.

Captain Edwards took a step forward. "Surely, you can find enough charity in your heart to spare me a short walk?" A bitter smile tugged at his lips as he waved his hat at the door. "It's not quite so busy there."

Her gut screamed 'no', but years of polite society prompted her to say, "Only a short walk, Captain. The children are waiting."

He didn't hide his relief. He bowed. "I thank you." He led her down the stairs to a side door near the kitchen that opened to the castle lawn.

As they stepped out into the bright, sunny day, Charlotte drew her pelisse close. "What do you wish to say?" she asked, once they'd gone a suitable distance from the door.

The Captain kept walking, and heaved a sigh, as if over-wrought with emotion.

Charlotte frowned but skipped to catch up with him. "Tell me, please." She glanced back at the castle and added, "My charges are waiting."

They neared the wall running along the cliff's edge. Did he intend to follow the path beyond the wall leading to the shore?

She stopped. "This is far enough, Captain Edwards. Say what you have to say and have done."

He halted and looked at her with such dejection that her heart twisted. She picked up her skirts and hurried to his side.

"Forgive me, Charlotte," he said.

"Forgive?" she repeated. There were so many things he *should* seek forgiveness for, she frankly didn't know of which one he spoke.

His eyes flicked past her. A shadow fell over his face, but before she could respond, he clamped a hand over her mouth.

Then her world went dark.

CHARLOTTE GROANED. HER HEAD THROBBED, HER BACK ACHED, and her limbs felt stiff and cold. She blinked into focus the dim light of a torch in an iron bracket bolted high on a rough stone wall. The smell of damp earth and the sea filled her nostrils as the rhythmic, distant roar of waves surrounded her.

She slowly sat up and pushed her tangled hair out of her face. It took a moment to recognize where she was. She sat on the floor of one of the sea caves. Charlotte froze. Captain Edward leaned against the cave wall directly across from her. Torchlight cast shadows on his face, making him appear large, formidable. He watched her with cold, glittering eyes.

"At last, you are awake," he said. "You made this difficult. It would have been so much easier if you had simply come to the stables after dinner last night, Charlotte."

Charlotte shook her head in confusion, then winced when the small movement sent a ripple of pain down her jaw. Understanding struck.

"*You* left the letter?"

He was a madman.

"You always walked the brazen side. It is time you learned your place, Charlotte." He crossed to where she sat on the ground. "You are weak. You need a man's strength. You will come to understand, one day, and thank me on your knees. I'm taking you from this place, willing or not. You are mine."

He grabbed her arm and yanked her to her feet. She tried to twist free. He drew back a hand and slapped her hard across the cheek. The sting splintered through her cheek. Tears sprang to her eyes.

"No other man may touch you," he snapped. "You kept me waiting too many years. It's high time you paid, and pay you shall, now that I see just how brazenly you behave with—"

With all her strength, she brought her knee up into his groin and shoved him back. He howled and stumbled backwards, arms flailing, then fell on the cave floor. Charlotte backed up and squinted in the darkness in search of the entrance. She had to go. *Now.* She hopped over his thrashing body and fled.

"Charlotte!" the Captain shouted in a strangled voice. "Come back here. That is an *order.*"

She tripped on the uneven cave floor and barely managed to catch herself before she fell. She pressed on. The dim torchlight soon faded and she stopped, surrounded by suffocating darkness. Her heart pounded. She was lost. She groped until her fingers contracted cold rock. Blindly, she felt her way forward. The dull, distant sound of crashing waves seemed to come from all sides.

"Charlotte," Captain Edwards' voice echoed.

Up ahead, a shaft of light streamed through an opening in the cavern ceiling above. Relief flooded. She lunged toward the light, but reached the spot to find that it was only a small hole in the ceiling. Tears slipped past her resolve, but she forced herself to continue.

"Charlotte," the Captain called again, this time, much closer.

She altered course and headed deeper into the caves.

"Answer me," Captain Edwards commanded.

The nearness of his voice sent a shiver down her spine. Faint light flickered on the wall.

"Stop this madness. Come here, at once!" he shouted.

A shaft of torchlight swept over the low, slanted ceiling above her. She caught sight of a jagged hole in the rock wall to the side. She raced to the small opening and fell to her knees. Frantically, she crawled through the opening into yet more darkness and stood. Fear stabbed. Stale air assaulted her nostrils. She reached out and gingerly trailed her fingers along the damp cave walls.

She'd taken no more than three steps when something unexpectedly brushed her face. She screeched and jumped back. Her foot slipped in loose gravel and she lost her balance. She pitched forward and her shin struck something hard as a burning shock of pain traveled from her ankle to her knee.

"Charlotte?" Captain Edwards' voice sounded so much closer now.

Torchlight fell through the passage.

CHAPTER 13

ALISTAIR STARED OUT HIS LIBRARY WINDOW. DARK GRAY CLOUDS covered the late afternoon sky. A cold, driving rain had brought an early evening, requiring that candles and lamps to be lit.

"I wager we will find your personal seal in Lady Cassilis's care." Nicholas stretched in the chair where he lounged before the fire.

Alistair shook his head. "I fail to see how she could have a hand in the matter. What does she have to gain by stealing my personal seal to falsify a note simply to send Charlotte to the stables? Nae. I fear it is another sort of mischief."

"Mischief." Nicholas' eyes lit. "I—"

"Uncle," a small voice gasped, "it's Charlotte."

Alistair looked around in alarm. Oliver stood by the door, bent over, holding his knees in an attempt to catch his breath. Mud stained the knees of his trousers and a stream of water dripped from his wet hair.

"What do you mean, lad?" Alistair crossed to him in three long strides. "Speak, at *once*."

"I can't find Miss Atchenson," Oliver gulped. "Anywhere."

Alistair forced himself to take a calming breath. The castle was large. She could be in the kitchens, or the library. "How long have you been searching?" he asked.

"Since afternoon tea," Oliver whispered. His face began to crumple. "I slipped away from Meg to find her. I have looked everywhere, Uncle. I thought she was taking too long to come back from seeing you. One of the maids said she saw her leave the castle with Captain Edwards, but I've—"

Captain Edwards? Alistair didn't hear the rest. He was already headed through the door.

In short order, he roused every man in the house, including the guests, and organized them into search parties. After dispatching them in all directions, he took command of the party to scour the sea caves and shore.

Cold rain drove down in icy sheets that stung his face as he lifted his oil lantern high and shouted for the men in his party to follow. He'd just turned to lead the way when a small figure darted through the rain and reached his side.

"Go back, Oliver," Alistair shouted over the wind and the shouts of the men behind him as they headed for the cliff trail.

The boy stubbornly shook his head. "No. I'm a Cassilis and I belong with the clan."

Alistair hesitated, then realized the boy was right. He clamped his hand down on the lad's shoulder and gave it a squeeze. "Stay near me. Understand?"

He nodded.

Facing the bitter winds head on, Alistair reached the slippery path that descended the cliffs to the rocky shore below. Behind him, the line of men with oil lanterns snaked down behind him. His mind raced.

Captain Edwards.

Cold anger seized Alistair's soul. He should've thought of the man sooner. No doubt, he was behind the forged letter, as well. He should have turned the man out of the house once he'd learned he was the captain Charlotte had been engaged to—be he Lady Brexley's chaperone or no.

They reached the shore and fanned out to scour area. Alistair led Oliver, Nicholas and a group of men over the rock pools toward the sea caves. Gusts of wind whistled through the yawing cave entrances like the ghostly skirl of pipes.

Alistair lifted his lantern high and picked a path over the boulders and sharp, jutting rocks until he stood, at last, in front of the ruined arched door that lead into the dark network of caverns beyond. He slowed and glanced at Oliver. The young lad stood strong and resolute. Pride flooded Alistair. The boy was a Cassilis, indeed.

The main chamber stood empty, as did the smaller chambers off to the side. As he wound his way up to the second level of caves, he spied a pin prick of light glancing off the ceiling ahead.

"There," he shouted to his men.

The light snuffed out, but he'd seen it. Alistair dashed forward with his men close behind.

"Charlotte!" he called as he ran, but only his own voice echoed back at him off the walls.

He ascended another level when a shout went up. Hope leapt in his chest. Sprinting forward, he caught sight of flickering light an instant before he rounded a corner. Alistair's heart fell. Two men dragged, not Charlotte, but Captain Edwards between them, his clothes torn and blood trickling down from a cut on his forehead.

An instant later, Alistair reached them. He seized the Edwards by the throat. "Where is she?" he snarled. "*Where?*"

The man's throat muscles struggled to work beneath his fingers. Alistair released his grip just enough to allow him to wheeze, "She ran, deeper into the caves."

It was all Alistair could do not to beat him to the ground. Alistair might need him in order to find Charlotte. Then...

"If one hair on her head is harmed, I will kill you." Alistair shoved him against the cave wall. "Hold him here," he thundered to his men.

He whirled and pushed deeper into the caves than he had ever been, Nicholas and Oliver close behind. He refused to think any harm might have befallen her. He called her name, again and again, with Oliver and Nicholas echoing her name as well.

Then he heard it. A small voice, panic-stricken and hysterical, emanated from the darkness ahead. "Alistair? *Alistair?*"

He raced ahead, Nicholas and Oliver on his heels, and burst into a small chamber.

"Alistair."

Her voice filtered through a small hole close to the ground. Alistair dropped to his knees and shone his light into a small chamber. He glimpsed the hem of her skirt. Fear twisted his belly. He was too large to fit through the opening. He glanced at Oliver, but discounted the idea.

"Can you come out?" he called to Charlotte.

She limped closer and fury swept through him when he realized she was injured. Alistair held his breath as she knelt. His light illuminated her face. Dried blood caked her face and hands.

"Is that really you, Alistair?" she whispered.

"Aye, love. Can you squeeze through the opening?"

She nodded and began to crawl through the hole. When she'd lifted herself out halfway, Alistair grasped her by the waist and pulled her up and into his arms.

"Captain Edwards—" she choked.

"Hush." Alistair stayed her with a soft kiss. "You need never see him again. He has been caught and will be turned over to the authorities."

She sagged in relief.

"What's this?" Nicholas asked.

Alistair glanced at Nicholas, who stood near the opposite side of the cavern, his torch illuminating a small, iron-banded chest with rusted hinges.

Oliver launched himself against Charlotte. "I was so worried about you, Miss."

She gave a half sob. "You're such a brave boy. What are you doing here?"

Alistair didn't miss the tremble in her voice.

Oliver drew back and stood straight. "I'm a Cassilis. I had to help with the search."

"You need to look at this, Alistair," Nicholas said with a long, low whistle.

He glanced at Nicholas. The baronet held an aged, oilskin package in his hands, his blue eyes wide with astonishment.

"Bring it," Alistair replied, then swung Charlotte up into his arms.

She was light as he carried her out of the caves with Oliver by his side. He hugged her close through the relentless rain. She clung to him until they reached the warmth of the castle. Once he'd settled her in a wingback chair in his library, he ordered the doctor summoned and stayed by her side as she looked up at him, her pupils large and dark in the library's soft light.

"The doctor will be here soon," he promised.

"There's little need for a doctor." She looked more like her old self. "I am fine."

He brought her fingers to his lips and smiled. "You have a fine black eye to prove it." He turned to Oliver and pointed to a plump footstool next to the opposite chair. "Bring me that stool, lad."

As the boy jumped to do his bidding, Alistair knelt and gently removed the slipper from her injured foot. He kissed the inside of her ankle, then carefully slid the stool in place.

She smiled, and the look in her eyes made his blood burn.

The doctor arrived, and Alistair left the man to tend to her injuries with Oliver by her side, while Alistair joined Nicholas at the desk. Nicholas didn't look up from the papers spread out before him.

"What is this?" Alistair asked as he halted beside the man's chair.

The baronet glanced at him. "I...don't know how to tell you," he replied in a solemn voice. "Other than to say..." His voice trailed away.

"Say what?" Alistair squinted over his shoulder at the papers on the desk.

Nicholas selected two aged sheets of parchment and held them out. "The piper's irrefutable proof," he said. "These are the papers that Lady Cassilis has been so desperately seeking."

Alistair froze.

"Nae, they're not," Oliver piped up from the chair near the fire. "She got her papers in the icehouse, Uncle."

Taking the papers from Nicholas, Alistair turned to his nephew. "The icehouse?" he asked. "What do you mean?"

The boy left Charlotte's side to join them at the desk, his eyes darting nervously from man to man.

"I will not thrash you, lad," Alistair promised, feeling drained. "The truth. I simply need the truth."

Oliver hesitated, then answered with a rush, "I followed her, Lady Cassilis, you know. You said to watch out for the man with the green hat. I saw him the first day when I went to the stables with Lady Cassilis. He dropped his hat near the kitchens. He's been here every day, wanting money and liquor. She called him Thomas." The boy looked up at him, his expression earnest.

It all began to make sense. Alistair exchanged a long look with Nicholas. They hadn't been asking the right person.

"What did they speak of at the icehouse that day? Thomas was there, was he not?"

"Yes." Oliver nodded. "I followed him from the kitchens. She came later. She wanted her papers. She's always talking about papers. She was angry he kept taking so long to fetch them and he demanded more money. He gave them to her at the icehouse and she left."

"What of the fire?" Alistair asked.

Oliver fidgeted a little before admitting, "After Lady Cassilis left, Thomas started drinking. I waited until he fell asleep and took his hat to show you, but he woke up, so I hid in the back. I waited and waited, but he kept drinking. I don't know how the fire started, but he had a lantern with him. I fell asleep, and when I woke up, the fire had started. I ran out as fast as I could."

"So, the drunken sot started the fire." Nicholas snorted.

"It would seem so." Alistair nodded, then addressed Oliver. "These papers he gave Lady Cassilis, what did they look like?"

"He gave her a leather package tied with red string. Said it came from the best scribes in Scotland."

Alistair looked at Nicholas. "No doubt, they are papers proving my birth as illegitimate, though coming from scribes, I wager they are forgeries."

To his surprise, Nicholas laughed. "I suspect you are right, but there's no need when you hold the answer to this riddle in your hand."

Alistair looked down at the parchment. The first sheet bore the Cassilis family crest emblazoned in the wax seal at the bottom of the page. He scanned the contents, surprised to discover it a certificate of his birth.

"The next paper," Nicholas said, "is a wee bit more interesting. Lady Cassilis won't like the tale those dates tell."

Alistair shuffled the papers and peered at the next sheet. A special license of marriage issued to his parents with a date a good year before his birth.

"You never were illegitimate," Nicholas murmured. "The piper's had this proof the entire time, hidden in the caves."

Alistair stared at the document in stunned disbelief. "So, the old earl wasn't referring to Foster," he whispered. "He spoke of the ghostly piper this entire time."

"Aye." Nicholas nodded at the remaining papers scattered on the desk. "You have always been the rightful heir to the title and the estates, and you were a good seven years of age when your mother died. The old earl's marriage to Lady Cassilis was never legal, lad. He needed her money, so he hid your existence with the ghostly piper and swept you away, as if you had never existed."

Alistair swallowed. "This castle consumed him." He glanced at the finery surrounding him. "There wasn't a thing he wouldn't have done to save his castle."

"Aye. Even sacrifice his firstborn as they do in the tales," the baronet commented with a shake of his dark head.

Alistair snorted and dropped the papers on the desk. "Then, we shall see this matter of Lady Cassilis settled once and for all."

A gleam of interest sparked Nicholas' eyes. "Shall I demand she turn the forged papers over at once?"

"Nae, do no' give her the chance to destroy them," Alistair replied. "Go to her rooms and find them yourself and take Foster with you."

"Even better." Nicholas grinned.

As he vanished through the door, Alistair turned to his young nephew still standing before him. Alistair ruffled the lad's hair. "You saved the day, lad, in more ways than one." He dropped his voice to a stern tone, "But enough wandering about the estate. You will stay out of mischief and learn your lessons like a proper gentleman."

"Aye, Uncle." The boy nodded, seriously.

They stared at each other, then Alistair's lip twitched into a proud smile and the boy suddenly turned away, but not before Alistair caught a glimpse of his mouth curving up in response. Alistair followed him back to Charlotte's side as the doctor stood to take his leave.

"Her injuries are minor, my lord." The doctor snapped his black case closed. "A few days' rest and she'll be back on her feet. I suggest she go straight to bed—now."

"I will see to it." Alistair smiled and squeezed Charlotte's shoulder. A rosy glow had returned to her cheeks.

He walked with the doctor to the door and assigned a footman to settle the bill. He'd just stepped back into the library when a screech shattered the air. He looked up. Lady Cassilis sailed down the corridor toward him, her thin jowls jiggling in rage. Nicholas followed sedately behind her. Alistair glanced at Charlotte and Oliver. The last thing he wanted was to subject them to another of Lady Cassilis's tantrums.

"I am owed an explanation on this matter. At once!" she shrilled. "My privacy has been violated by this ruffian." She swept into the library with Nicholas on her heels, carrying a leather package tied with red string. "That is mine," Lady Cassilis hissed. "I demand you return it. At once."

Alistair closed the door. "Is it yours? Be careful what you say, Lady Cassilis."

She whirled, eyes flashing. "Yes, it is mine." Her voice gained strength as her thin nostrils flared. "It is your undoing, Alistair. It is the irrefutable proof."

Nicholas crossed to the desk and dropped his package next to the piper's papers.

"This estate was never yours, Alistair," she snapped. "In fact, according to what I have found, you might very well not even be the earl's son."

Alistair raked his fingers through his hair and hazarded a look at Charlotte and Oliver. Charlotte faced the fire, Oliver in her lap. Appreciation flooded him. She was staying out of sight. He couldn't blame her. She had no wish to face Lady Cassilis.

He returned his attention to the older woman. He wanted this matter finished. "Irrefutable proof? I shall be delighted to offer your papers, along with mine, to the full scrutiny of the court. I ride for Glasgow tomorrow to present them both."

She blinked. "Both? Of what do you speak?"

He nodded at the desk. "This night's unfortunate events uncovered proof of a different kind, Lady Cassilis, one buried deep in the piper's sea caves."

She went rigid.

"Shall I show her?" Nicholas queried softly.

Alistair nodded, once.

The baronet picked up the marriage license and extended it toward her. Her gaze locked on the paper. Her expression shifted from a blank expression to one of deep, dark rage.

Her hands began to shake. *"How could he?"*

So, she'd noticed the dates. Alistair eyed her grimly. "I quite agree with your sentiments. How could my own father deny me and my mother? How could he allow you to treat me in such an ignoble, base manner, a wee, frightened child of no more than seven years?"

She jerked and fell back a step.

"It's over, Lady Cass—" he broke off. "Perhaps, I should no longer call you that, for you were never a Cassilis."

Her chin began to tremble. "You wrong me cruelly. Just like your father before you. What will you do now? He ripped away every penny I had. I have nothing. *Nothing.* Not even the monies that were to be set aside for my old age. Do you wish to see me penniless? Do you wish me to beg bread by the roadside?"

A nerve twitched in Alistair's cheek. The woman had caused so much pain, and she'd clearly bought forged documents to steal his estate—and now she expected mercy? He was too tired to care. He strode to the desk. Nicholas handed him the marriage license and he gathered the piper's papers along with the forged ones and dumped them back into the chest.

"Retire to your rooms and stay there until I call for you."

"I didn't turn the papers in, Alistair," she wailed, then collapsed to the floor, weeping hysterically. "You cannot ruin me, not over that. I kept the papers in my desk. I didn't turn them in." She kept weeping, insisting she'd done no wrong as he ordered several footmen to carry her away.

"Poor sod, your father, to voluntarily wed that," Nicholas said with a low whistle when the door finally closed behind them.

Alistair snorted. "Never did a man deserve it more. He ruined us both through his greed."

His friend cocked a brow. "Will you show mercy?"

What would he do? He rubbed his eyes. The thought of dragging Lady Cassilis to court was unbearable. "I have nothing to fear from her now. She has no choice but to behave, now that I have proof she'll never want exposed to the light of day."

Nicholas let out a long sigh. "Then send her far away. Far, far away, or we'll never have a moment's peace."

"Aye." An idea caught his fancy. "Methinks Lady Prescott would enjoy her company. She wouldn't dare refuse, not when she's been living in my London townhouse rent free."

His friend belted a hearty laugh. "Never did two women deserve each other more."

Alistair smiled and faced Charlotte. She peered around the chair at him. The admiration in her eyes made his blood sing.

"Aye," he said softly, speaking to her with his eyes. "I am done with Lady Cassilis and all the rest. I have other things to think of now."

CHAPTER 14

AFTER SEEING HIS STEPMOTHER ON HER WAY TO LONDON AND Captain Edwards bundled off to the authorities, Alistair left for Glasgow to submit the Piper's proof to the courts and settle the matter of his inheritance once and for all. It took longer than he liked. The wheels of the law turned slowly but, at last, he saw the matter done, and he left Glasgow, eager to return to Castle Culzean and the hazel-eyed lass who awaited him.

When, at last, he drove down the tree-lined carriage drive and under Culzean's arched entrance, he discovered his barouche was only one of many gathered there.

"The spring ball is tomorrow," Nicholas greeted him with a grin as he stepped out of his carriage. "I feared you, the guest of honor, had forgotten."

"If I had organized it myself, I would have remembered," Alistair said as he and Nichols entered the rear gardens. The castle glittered with lights and guests milled about the lawn to the accompaniment of a small orchestra.

"Did you not say the party was tomorrow?" Alistair asked.

"Many of the guests arrived early, my dear fellow."

"Will they be leaving soon?" Alistair half growled as he took a glass of champagne from the tray of a passing waiter. He emptied the glass then handed it to another waiter and navigated past a group of ladies in a rainbow array of elegant evening gowns with Nicholas close behind. He sidestepped a group of men, then entered the castle through the open balcony doors and strode across the ballroom.

Alistair glanced at Nicholas. "Hadn't you better see to your guests?"

"Later."

They reached a side staircase and sprinted up the stairs. At last, they reached the study.

A maid poked the fire in the hearth. "It's good to have you back, my lord." She leaned the poker against the hearth, then bobbed a curtsey and hurried out the door.

With a sigh, Alastair rubbed his shoulder, then noticed a parcel on the table.

"That came with the post a few days ago." Nicholas plopped down in a chair and stretched out his long legs.

Alistair pulled back the wrapper to reveal a worn, leather-bound book. As he lifted it up, a sheet of paper fell out, fluttering to the floor. He picked it up, then scanned the bold script that stated the book was the authentic possession of one Anna Atchenson, Charlotte's mother.

"What book is this?" Nicholas asked curiously from his seat before the fire.

Alistair shook his head. "It's not a book, lad, 'tis a treasure of the heart." He slipped the book back into the wrapping and tied the string as Nicholas averted his gaze to the fire. Something about the man's manner caught his attention.

Alistair set the package back on the desk. "What ill has befallen you? You do not seem like yourself."

"I am well enough," he replied with a pained look.

Alistair grimaced. "Please assure me you haven't invited new house guests I must attend to?"

Nicholas humphed. "I may have landed myself in a wee bit of trouble."

"How is this new?" Alistair couldn't resist a bit of a mocking laugh.

Nicholas made a half-hearted attempt to smile before saying, "It's blackmail."

"Blackmail?" Alistair's amusement faded. "That sounds serious. Who?"

"A woman." The baronet scowled.

So soon? But then, Nicholas had lost interest in Lady Catherine Brexley from the moment of her arrival. He'd been outright relieved when she'd gone. After the scandal of her chaperone, Captain Edwards, had come to light, she'd fled Culzean as if from the bubonic plague.

Alistair regarded him. "A woman? Then I daresay it's well deserved."

Nicholas shot him a scathing look, then hefted himself to his feet and stalked from the room. Alistair watched him go, but shrugged the matter away. Nicholas and scandals went hand-in-hand. Picking up the wrapped book, he smiled. Since he'd left, he'd thought of little else other than Charlotte. Now, there was nothing to stop him.

The setting sun cast long shadows over the castle as he took the rear stairs up to the nursery. In the distance, he heard the gong of the dinner bell mingling with the strains of a waltz played by the musicians out on the lawn. He strode down the hall, past the maids lighting the candles and lamps, and reached the nursery door.

Slowly, he twisted the knob and opened the door. Charlotte stood at the window. Music drifted through the open window. He slid his gaze down her slender body. The ever-defiant curls escaped the pins above the curve of her neck. He'd missed her.

He crept into the room and carefully set the package on the table before tiptoeing to stand behind her and slide his hands around her waist. She started, but he quickly pulled her against his chest, then dropped light kisses on the curve of her neck. Her pulse quickened beneath his lips.

He inhaled the perfume of her hair, whispered, "I've missed you."

She tensed. "My—"

"Alistair," he cut her off. "*My* Alistair."

"My Alistair," she repeated with a breath of a laugh.

His name upon her lips sent a shiver of desire through him. He sucked her earlobe between his teeth. She shuddered.

"Say, 'my darling Alistair.' I like that even more," he murmured.

She laughed and, suddenly, he wanted more of her. He pulled pins from her hair, freeing her silken curls to tumble over her shoulders, then turned her in his arms. He took her lips in a sweet kiss, tender and passionate. She closed her eyes and moaned. She fit him perfectly.

He broke the kiss, then tenderly kissed each of her eyelids, and said, "I must ruin this time between us."

She went rigid, her full, dark lashes flying open in alarm.

"Hush," he assured her quickly. He rubbed his cheek against hers. "I merely meant these moments of intimacy…will now be more difficult. When an official courtship begins, they will hound us with chaperones. They will expect things done in a proper fashion."

She didn't relax as expected and, to his surprise, she flattened her palms on his chest and pushed him back. "How can I allow you to court me? Lady Cassilis was right."

He lifted a brow. "Now that is a name I didn't expect to hear." He gathered her close in his arms once again. "Pray tell, what did she say?"

"There are those born to sit in the Blue Drawing Room," she whispered, her hazel eyes large, "and those who are born to clean it."

He studied her face, searching for the right words, then the soft refrain of a waltz filtered through the window. He smiled, then whirled with her in his arms.

Alistair nuzzled her ear. "That may very well be, my dear. But it matters little, for you were born to dance in it." He kissed her again, tenderly, then slowly stepped back. "Please, Charlotte, accept me. Accept my courtship. Dance with me tomorrow in the ball. Wear your dress, your crimson gown. I beg you." Her brow wrinkled, signaling a response he surely wasn't inclined to hear. He shook his head. "Think on it. Give our love a chance, Charlotte. I will not hear your answer tonight."

He planted a kiss on the top of her head, then left with a heavy heart, fearing she would, indeed, refuse him on the morrow.

THE DAY OF THE BALL DAWNED. MORE GUESTS ARRIVED, MAKING Alistair feet like a stranger in his own home. He escaped the whirlwind of color, music and lights to brood in his study. Charlotte had yet to hunt him down and give him her answer. Was the delay a good sign? A bad one? Was she avoiding him? She must have decided to refuse him and, if so, how could he change her mind?

Sometime later in the afternoon, a brooding Nicholas arrived at his door. "What ails you?" he asked, inviting himself in to sit before the fire.

Alistair heaved a sigh. "Last night, I asked Charlotte for the honor of courting her." When the baronet didn't reply, he glanced up to find the man staring at the fire, lost in thought.

"There's little cause for you to fret, my dear fellow. It's plain for all to see you are besotted with one another."

It was a heartening answer. Still, he found it hard to let

himself be comforted. "I fear she is trapped by the rules of society."

"Trapped," Nicholas repeated in a rough voice.

Alistair cocked his head to one side. "How goes it with you? Is this woman still hellbent on blackmail?"

"Woman?" his friend exploded. "Nae, she is more of a scheming, twisted *she-devil*." He closed his eyes and added so softly that Alistair could scarcely hear him, "I'll handle it. I always do."

"Aye," Alistair replied, but when Nicholas refused to explain further, he let his thoughts wander once again to Charlotte.

Was it good…or bad that she hadn't yet arrived to speak with him?

Nicholas stood. "We make a merry pair, hiding in the study on the day of a grand ball. Come, let's busy ourselves away from our thoughts."

Against his better judgement, Alistair followed.

The afternoon passed first in a series of card games, but exactly who won or lost, Alistair couldn't say. He sat in the Blue Drawing Room, pretending to listen to a pianoforte performance by the talented Lady Crenshaw, but his thoughts were on the laughing hazel eyes of a lass who could swear like a sailor.

Dinner arrived, a parade of soups, jellies, creams, good hams from Yorkshire, casseroles, roasts, puddings, cheeses, lemon ice, rose soufflé cakes on elevated stands, wine, claret, whisky—and much more. He couldn't recall tasting even one bite.

With dinner over, the guests filtered into the spacious ball-room with its polished floor, brocade and gold taffeta draped windows, and its pale blue walls trimmed with gilded frieze. Full-sized oil paintings depicting various Cassilis earls hung between heavy mirrors in ornate gilded frames. Venetian cut-glass and silver chandeliers hung from the painted ceilings, the room brilliant with thousands of glistening candles reflecting in the mirrors like stars. Footmen bearing silver trays passed among the guests as couples stepped onto the dance floor and began to swirl around the room in a blur of sparkling jewels and color.

The musicians played.

The dancers danced.

Alistair left the ballroom and wandered the corridors, hungry for any sign of Charlotte among the guests who milled in those areas, but found none.

The hour grew late.

His despair increased with each passing moment. Charlotte would refuse him. He knew that now. She would let society dictate her happiness. Did she not think him worth the effort? Perhaps, he should have tracked her down. But he knew that was wrong. Any answer she gave under duress would not come from her heart. Worse, if he pushed her away… He couldn't bear the thought. What if she'd left in an effort to escape his attentions? He strode down the hallway toward the front entrance. Turning a corner, he slowed his step. God help him, guests had gathered in the foyer. One man even stood on the lowest step of the grand staircase and leaned a hip against the banister.

Alistair's heart pounded. He turned back the way he'd come and started—

A heavy hand clamped down on his shoulder. Alistair whirled.

Nicholas' hand fell away. Eyes sparking with dry amusement, he said, "Why the long face?"

The man knew right well enough. Alistair turned, but the baronet grabbed his shoulder again.

"Nicholas," Alistair snarled.

His friend's grip tightened and he spun Alistair around and

chuckled into his ear, "There is your answer, my friend." He nodded in the direction of the oval grand staircase.

Alistair froze. Charlotte descended the stairs, a vision in a high-waisted gown of crimson silk, enriched with a fine needlework display of glittering silver and seed pearls. Long gloves encased her slender arms, rising within an inch of her sheer cap sleeves trimmed with rosettes. Already, the rebellious curls he loved so much had escaped the gold band in her hair and twined around the base of her slender neck.

The soft, sensuous folds of her skirt and the hint of cleavage revealed by her scooped neckline drew his gaze an instant before she reached the landing and he locked his gaze with hers.

CHAPTER 15

THE COOKERY BOOK HAD SEALED HER FATE. THE MOMENT Charlotte untied the strings and the paper fell away, she had fallen to her knees in tears. The man owned her heart. Accept him? With the honor she knew lived in his soul, how could she not? And his kiss? Her lips still burned and her body still ached for his touch.

She'd spent the entire day listening to Meg's wise advice as she'd modeled the crimson ballgown for the dressmaker's last-minute alterations. Oliver had watched in quiet, solid approval while Jane had danced around the nursery from pure excitement.

It was later than they all liked before they finally twirled her around for the final inspection. Pleased with their handiwork, they escorted her to the top of the oval grand staircase and watched as she stood nervously with her hand on the rail and one slippered foot poised to take the very first step.

"Go, lass," Meg encouraged.

Charlotte glanced over her shoulder at Oliver and Jane, who poked their heads through the railing, grins wide, as Meg stood behind them. Charlotte took a deep breath and stared at the swirl of color and glittering diamonds of the world below her, a world so foreign it froze her feet to the landing. Then she saw him. He stood, Nicholas' hand on his shoulder.

Her heart dropped. She'd hoped to have a few more minutes to steady herself. How could she ever steady herself while in his presence? He stood so tall, so devastatingly handsome in his velvet cutaway coat, snowy, starched white shirt, elegantly knotted gray silk cravat and a lustrous black silk waistcoat.

The guests faded away and, gaze locked on the man who had stolen her heart, she descended, the yards of soft crimson silk floating around her ankles like a cloud.

He turned suddenly.

Her legs weakened.

He stared, unmoving.

Her heart began to pound. Did he not want to see her? Had he changed his mind? Had she miscalculated?

Charlotte reached the landing.

Fear knotted her stomach. He still hadn't moved.

A look of wonder crossed his face. He pushed past Nicholas and, an instant later, stood before her. He captured her hand and brought it to his mouth. The gentle kiss he pressed to her fingers was so…reverential. Tears sprang to her eyes.

Charlotte drew a shaky breath and whispered, "If I snuffle the soup and drink the rose water, it is on your head." She winced at the nervous, strangled sound of her voice. "And heaven help me if I swear."

His eyes softened. "I am the envy of every man in this room —in the world." He placed her fingers over his heart and whispered, "I love you."

His beautiful green eyes seared her soul. Mesmerized, she traced the dimple in his chin with a fingertip and whispered, "I love you more."

"Propriety be damned," he growled low in his chest as his

pupils darkened with desire. His chiseled lips curved into a smile, and he added in soft warning, "I fear we may be wed scandalously soon after this, my dear."

Before she could ask, he gathered her close, crushed her against his broad chest, and took her lips in a ravenous kiss.

SNEAK PEEK AT A STRANGER'S KISS

LORDS OF CHANCE BOOK TWO

TARAH SCOTT

CHAPTER 1

OLIVIA SLAMMED HER GLASS OF LEMONADE DOWN ON THE TABLE. The *cad*. Had he no shame? He was *her* fiancé—or would be soon. Yet there he was, Timothy Menzies, pulling Maggie Wilkins behind the hawthorn hedgerow in Lady Blair's garden.

"Olivia, darling, do you have any more *Summertime Melody* books? The one with the new arrangement of *Robin Adair?*" Lady Kendrick called out as Olivia stormed past the summer tent spread out on the lawn.

"Louisa sang so wonderfully this afternoon," another voice chimed amidst choruses of agreement.

Then, of course, the inevitable murmurings, all a variation of, "Isn't that the Mad Printer's daughter?"

Olivia rolled her eyes and continued on as if she hadn't heard. Right now, she was keen on giving the two-timing Timothy Menzies a piece of her mind. Questions of song and everything else could wait.

With a scowl, she marched around the hedgerow. She was treated to an impressive view of Lady Blair's stately Wedderburn Manor, a majestic backdrop to the formal garden that sprawled before her in a fine array of climbing roses, lilacs, and sculpted boxwoods.

At first, she couldn't spot him, but the shaking limbs of a boxwood to the left drew her attention. Timothy. Not more than a dozen yards away behind a marble Italian bust. He stood with an awkward arm locked around Maggie's waist and his lips attached to hers like a leech. Olivia huffed. Just what did Maggie have that she didn't? They were practically twins—both redheads with bright green eyes and voluptuous curves.

As if sensing her eyes burning holes through his head, Timothy turned and squinted in her direction. He froze.

Olivia's nostrils flared.

He cringed, looking as guilty as sin.

Olivia's emotions churned. She couldn't lose him—not that she loved him, of course—but now with her father disabled, she needed a husband. Desperately. Her father's music shop stood on the brink of ruin and now that the bankers understood he'd never recover, they had given Olivia an ultimatum: sell the shop or hand it over to a husband, as a proper woman should.

Unfortunately, finding a husband had proved a daunting challenge. Timothy, as the fourth son of a bookbinder, had been her best possibility, by far. He could scarcely do better than to marry her. She could tolerate him—barely.

Yet, as she saw him, his arm hooked around Maggie's waist —of all women, *why her?* —a sense of anger warred with hurt pride.

The anger won.

With a scowl, Olivia planted her hands on her hips. Her left elbow struck something that gave way only slightly.

A harsh intake of breath behind her made her realize she'd just elbowed the gut of a passing stranger.

"Pardon me," she tossed a distracted apology over her shoulder.

"My pleasure, I assure you," a man's deep baritone rumbled above her left ear, much higher than she usually heard.

He had to be tall. Timothy was short and incredibly sensitive over the matter. Without a second thought, Olivia whirled, grabbed the stranger by his neckcloth, rose on her tiptoes and planted a kiss over his startled lips. He was even taller than she expected. She would have missed his mouth entirely and kissed his chin instead had he not obligingly dipped the last inch or two.

The subtle blend of soap and sandalwood eddied around her. Then, the man's lips parted beneath hers. Surprised, Olivia dropped to her heels. His head dipped with her, never breaking contact as his tongue teased the seam of her lips. Instinct opened her mouth. His tongue immediately slid over hers. The soft warmth along with the roughness of his chin sent a frisson of awareness straight down to her toes.

Startled, Olivia's lashes flew open. Just when had she closed them? And was this even a kiss? She'd never experienced shivers in other parts of her body when Timothy had dropped a peck on her mouth.

Flustered, she wrenched free of the man and stepped back. She caught only the briefest impression of blond hair, laughing gray eyes, and a strong, dimpled chin before he'd caught her about the waist and swung her back into the circle of his arms.

"Have a care, lass." His chest vibrated against her breasts.

He stepped back, pulling her with him as a footman barreled around the hedgerow behind them. The footman gasped and lifted his tray of lemon ices over Olivia's head. He danced sideways. The crystal glasses clinked and wobbled precariously as he attempted to regain his balance.

He succeeded. Barely. With a deep breath, he schooled his features and politely dipped his chin. "Pardon me, my lord, miss."

"Bravo, well done," the man holding Olivia commended with a chuckle.

With a formal nod, the footman spun smartly on his heel and hurried off toward the tent.

The hard muscles beneath Olivia shifted. She held still, acutely aware of a hard abdomen, long thighs, and the defined muscles of the arm so casually looped around her waist. Her heart skipped a beat as every nerve in her body flared to life. She'd never known such intimate contact with a man could have such a heightening effect. The experience was far different than she'd imagined.

"It's been a pleasure, Miss," the man began.

Embarrassed, she twisted free of his embrace, and then suddenly remembered Timothy. A quick glance toward the hedgerow revealed both Timothy and his redheaded lover had gone.

"I daresay, you succeeded in making the sallow-faced fop jealous," the man behind her commented in a knowing voice.

Fop? Olivia winced. The description fit Timothy more than she cared to admit. Still, she tossed her head and lifted her chin. "I wait for no one. I was merely illustrating that fact. He's no longer welcome to keep my company, good sir."

She faced the man then, and for the first time, noticed the fine quality of his immaculate white shirt, gray silk cravat, and double-breasted, velvet-trimmed waistcoat. Expensive and of the highest quality. The clothes of a nobleman.

Wincing, she hastily amended, "Eh…my lord."

Again, he chuckled, the sound drawing her eyes from his midriff to his face. Sweet Lord above, the man was handsome. He towered over her, his gray eyes glinting with amusement over his strong, straight nose. Then, her gaze dropped to his lips. They appeared as sensual as they'd felt. She shivered.

A light summer breeze blew through the garden, ruffling

his blond hair as he peered down at her with brow cocked. "Only a fool would risk losing a lass like you." His lip quirked.

Olivia's eyes widened.

"Aye, a true man doesn't let the lass that caught his interest slip through his fingers. He goes after her." His lips widened into a mischievous grin, then he lowered his voice to add, "Rather like this."

Before she could respond, he caught her close. His fingers splayed low over the base of her spine as he molded her body against his. A wave of liquid heat flooded straight to her core as his tongue immediately sought entry to her mouth. She didn't hesitate. She opened her lips, breathing him in as he swept inside. For a timeless moment, their tongues tangled. Warm. Wet. She dug her fingers into his waistcoat to steady herself. He moaned, a soft sound, more intimate than she'd ever heard, and then, slowly, he pulled away.

"Aye, lass." His laugh was a lazy one, full of satisfaction. "A true man kisses the woman he's interested in—precisely like that."

He stepped away, executed a gallant bow, swung on his heel, and strode through the garden toward the gray stone manor without a backward glance.

Dazed, Olivia watched him go, unable to tear her gaze from his narrow hips and the line of his broad shoulders. Lord help her, but after him, how could she ever make peace with Timothy's fumbling pecks and awkward, one-armed hugs? Who knew such kisses truly existed outside the pages of a book?

"Olivia?"

Startled, Olivia jerked as her friend, Louisa, joined her.

Beautiful Louisa Hamilton, a well-endowed opera singer with a lark's voice and a body that drove men mad, knew how to use both of her assets to her advantage. She smiled at Olivia, every strand of her elaborately coifed, raven hair in place and each fold of her rose satin gown artfully arranged.

Olivia nodded a greeting, ignoring the customary twinge of envy she felt in Louisa's presence. She'd never attain such elegance and beauty. She simply hadn't the time nor patience to primp for hours in front of the mirror, painstakingly painting her face, even to the darkening of each individual eyelash.

"Did you find him?" Louisa's brown eyes sparkled with anticipation.

Olivia frowned, puzzled. "Who?"

Louisa covered her mouth with her hands and giggled. "Your lips are swollen. He kissed you, didn't he? A real kiss this time. I *knew* he couldn't resist you in that green gown."

Olivia blinked and glanced down at the green-sprigged muslin she'd borrowed from Louisa just that morning.

"There's no need to be shy," Louisa chided. "Tell me, Olivia. Do. I didn't think Timothy knew *how* to kiss."

He obviously didn't—not if one could call what the nobleman had done a kiss. Olivia shook her head, finding the experience far too intense to share, especially with Louisa. Glasgow's gossips would be chattering about the Mad Printer's lusty daughter within the hour. Maybe even less.

"Oh, fiddlesticks." Louisa rolled her eyes and gave Olivia's arm a disappointed tug. Then, her face brightened. "Don't fret. I'll pull each delicious detail from your lips at my house party."

Again, Olivia shook her head. "I really must return to the shop."

"Nonsense. You are coming," Louisa announced firmly. "I sang your songs, did I not?"

Olivia clenched her jaw. She'd hardly sung the songs for free. While they were friends, they weren't of the bosom buddy kind. She'd paid Louisa a fine penny to sing and she had the contracts safely tucked away under the print shop's floorboards as proof—but disagreeing with Louisa was always a losing proposition. The opera singer altered facts to suit her fancy.

Still, Olivia simply wasn't in the mood to attend a party—especially one of Louisa's raucous ones. "I can't."

"They never rush to the print shop to buy the sheet music *this* quickly, silly," Louisa reproved in a teasing tone. "But even if they should, you still have your shop boy, don't you?"

"William?" Olivia grimaced. She struggled to keep shop boys. She'd hired William only a month ago and had already caught him sleeping on the press room floor in the broad light of day nearly a dozen times. Still, as lazy as he was, he was the only one she could afford. "Yes, he's there," she muttered, then with a roll of her eyes, added, "And perhaps even awake."

Louisa snorted. "Just come for an hour or two, and then I'll have my coachman take you home. No doubt, you'll arrive at the same time as if you'd walked."

That made Olivia smile. Her feet still ached from the morning's trip. She gave in with a sigh. "Very well."

"Then I'll say my farewells as you jot down your music orders. Let's meet at my carriage, say, in half an hour?"

Olivia nodded and Louisa dashed away across the expanse of green lawn with a lightness in her step that indicated a man was involved. Olivia pursed her lips, a little jealous. Louisa never lacked for suitors, though none had, as yet, proposed marriage. Not that Timothy had, despite the number of times Olivia had prodded him.

She scowled, irritated to find herself hunting for a husband yet again. The bankers had agreed to meet her next week—wanting an introduction to her fiancé. Perhaps she'd pushed Timothy too fast…

Irritated, she blew her hair out of her face, opened her reticule and fished out her pencil along with a sheet of paper. Time to work. The charity event had entered the tea-drinking stage, the time when the attendees relaxed with their cups of

Pekoe and gossiped about the afternoon's performance behind their fans. Today, they would have little to critique. Louisa had delivered a fine performance. So fine, in fact, that Olivia wondered if she'd printed enough copies of *Robin Adair*.

Teacups clinked, and the scent of lilacs swirled around Olivia as she entered the tent.

"Olivia, darling, do tell me you have the version of *Robin Adair* that Miss Hamilton sang."

"I would so love a copy as well, my dear. Have your shop boy run the music over in the morning, will you?"

Olivia moved as quickly as she could through the tables, recording names and bobbing curtsies along the way. As she'd thought, requests for *Robin Adair* outnumbered all others, and this time, she heard the "Ah, the mad printer's daughter again, aye?" comments only twice. Not that such comments bothered her anymore. She was simply far too busy. She had a print shop to run, an infirm father to care for, and bills to pay.

When she finished her rounds, she tucked her paper and pencil back into her reticule and headed toward Lady Blair's table to bid her farewell.

The Lady Blair of Wedderburn Manor sat at the tent's edge near the lilacs, relaxing comfortably in her latticework chair and chatting with Glasgow's premiere gossip, the Lady Kendrick. Though both women were of the same age, Lady Blair seemed far younger. Even though her face lacked wrinkles and her figure rivaled the season's slender debutantes, her perpetual youth stemmed more from the kindness of her heart than any physical attribute.

Lady Kendrick, on the other hand, though rail thin, twitched and fidgeted in a manner that reminded Olivia of a mouse. Today, dressed in a brown gown adorned with drooping gray feathers, Olivia couldn't help but think she resembled one.

As Lady Blair's distinct silvery laughter filtered through the tent, Olivia paused. How many times had she stood in this exact spot and listened to Lady Blair laugh with her very own dear mother, the disowned Lady Glenna of Lennox? Of all her mother's friends, only Lady Blair had remained at her mother's side and helped her through the pain she'd endured from her family over daring to wed her true love—a poor music publisher's son with no title--instead of her family's choice of groom. Only Lady Blair had continued to invite her mother to Wedderburn Manor for tea, even after her father, the Duke of Lennox, disowned her and proclaimed his younger daughter, Arlene, his heir. He'd announced his decision during a lavish ball and publicly bestowed upon Arlene the famed Lennox Blue Slipper, as family tradition dictated.

"THE BLUE SLIPPER WAS TO HAVE BEEN YOURS, GLENNA." LADY BLAIR frowned as she poured the tea.

"Nonsense. I would have made a dismal Duchess." Olivia's mother had laughed, then smiled at Olivia where she played near the lilacs. "Anyway, what need have I for a sapphire slipper? I have the wealth of the world, right there, in a little sprite with ink-stained hands."

Lady Blair waved for Olivia to join them.

"She takes after her father, so very much. I swear she already knows how to operate the printing press better than he does...."

OLIVIA CLOSED HER EYES AND DREW A DEEP BREATH. SHE MISSED her mother. So much. The nearly four years since the carriage accident had been hard ones.

She brushed the tears collecting at the corners of her eyes, lifted her lashes and forced her feet forward.

"They say Lord Randall is desperate," Lady Kendrick was saying as Olivia arrived. "He must find a rich wife and soon, but with a temper as black as a chimney sweeper's feet…well, I wish him luck."

Lady Blair graciously dipped her head. "I knew him as a child. He grew up with my dear Nicholas."

"Well, what can I say?" Lady Kendrick lowered her voice, "They say Lord Randall's been keeping company with those opera singers—and *more* than one." The mousy woman's nose twitched as her lips quivered in a salacious smile.

Olivia lifted a brow. Lord help her, the only things the woman lacked were whiskers and a tail.

Lady Blair's face brightened as Olivia arrived. "Olivia, child. I've missed you so."

"Lady Blair, Lady Kendrick." Olivia curtsied deeply. She'd spent the past fifteen minutes bobbing up and down for the sake of a sale, but this time, she meant every inch of respect as she curtsied low before Lady Blair.

"Come now, Olivia," Lady Blair admonished as she grasped Olivia's forearm and lifted her upright. "You're the daughter of my dearest friend, and if I may say so, the daughter I wish I had."

Again, tears misted Olivia's lashes.

Lady Blair squeezed her arm in silent sympathy, and then let her go. "Unfortunately, you've just missed my dear Nicholas. He's off to Edinburgh, again. I would so love the two of you to meet."

Olivia smiled. Poor Lady Blair. Her son was well-known as a notorious rake. Not for the first time, she wondered how such a lovely woman could produce such a son. "Perhaps another time, my lady," she demurred.

"Yes, yes, my dear." Lady Blair sighed, then smiled. "Perhaps he can join us in Glasgow for your event. What was it called? Ah yes, *An Enchanted Summer Evening*. When will the tickets be sold?"

The question elicited a small rush of excitement. One more

payment to the Theater Royale and then, finally, Glasgow would hear her father's music: *An Enchanted Summer Evening*, songs by Oliver Mackenzie. There would be no 'Mad Printer' comments after that. Glasgow would stand in awe, and since she'd be the only publisher to print the music, she'd finally free the shop from debt.

"Soon, my lady," Olivia promised.

"Pray tell, you're not encouraging this foolish venture, Lady Blair?" a testy voice rasped from behind.

Lady Blair rose swiftly to her feet. "Your Grace," she murmured, her eyes locked over Olivia's shoulder.

Olivia turned as a craggy-faced man with salt-and-pepper hair joined them, tall and distinguished in his green plaid kilt. Judging from his black brows drawn into a scowl and the way his jaw jutted, he was greatly displeased.

Olivia dropped a quick curtsey and began backing away.

The man's eyes narrowed into slits. "Olivia," he grated, his lips barely opening as if speaking through clenched teeth.

Olivia blinked. He knew her name? She'd never met him in her life. He was obviously wealthy, a noble of repute. The smallest of the rings glittering on his knobby fingers stood testament to his wealth. Never had she seen so large a sapphire. No doubt, he mistook her for someone else.

"My lord," she murmured, inching away.

"Olivia," he said again.

Bobbing again, Olivia cast a puzzled glance at Lady Blair for guidance, but to her shock, Lady Blair appeared almost stricken. A meadowlark landed in the lilacs behind her, its chirp unnaturally loud in the silence that had fallen over the tent.

"Olivia," the stern man repeated.

With growing consternation, Olivia faced the man again. His eyes, so very green and so very cold, narrowed as she frowned. "My lord?"

When he didn't answer, Lady Blair cleared her throat. "My dear Olivia, may I introduce His Grace, the Duke of Lennox."

Lennox. Olivia stared into the man's eyes for a full five seconds before recognition struck.

Lennox. *The* Duke of Lennox.

Lord save her.

He was her grandfather.